Meet Jessica and Elizabeth Wakefield

Created by
Francine Pascal

BANTAM BOOKS
NEW YORK • TORONTO • LONDON • SYDNEY • AUCKLAND

MEET JESSICA AND ELIZABETH WAKEFIELD
A Bantam Book / June 1994

Sweet Valley Kids™, *Sweet Valley Twins and Friends*®
Sweet Valley High® and *Sweet Valley University*™
are trademarks of Francine Pascal.

Conceived by Francine Pascal

Produced by Daniel Weiss Associates, Inc.
33 West 17th Street
New York, NY 10011

ISBN: 0-553-56716-0

Published simultaneously in the United States and Canada

Bantam Books are published by Bantam Books, a division of Bantam
Doubleday Dell Publishing Group, Inc. Its trademark, consisting of the
words "Bantam Books" and the portrayal of a rooster, is Registered in U.S.
Patent and Trademark Office and in other countries. Marca Registrada.
Bantam Books, 1540 Broadway, New York, New York 10036.

PRINTED IN THE UNITED STATES OF AMERICA

OPM 0 9 8 7 6 5 4 3 2 1

PART ONE

Hi! I'm Elizabeth Wakefield. If you're interested in learning about Sweet Valley, California, the most beautiful place on earth, believe me, I have plenty to say. And that's not just because I want to be a writer, and having lots to say is my business. You see, I grew up in Sweet Valley, on Calico Drive, with my mom and dad, my older brother, Steven, and—most importantly—my twin sister, Jessica.

A lot of you may know Jessica. If there's a party within fifty miles, you can count on her showing up. But don't expect her to be on time, because if there's one thing Jessica believes in, it's being fashionably late! I'm more likely to arrive fifteen minutes early, hopefully in time to

1

help the hostess with last-minute details. But that's just one of the differences between Jessica and me. . . .

I'll tell you more about Jessica and me later. First I want to tell you about Sweet Valley. I've been to the English countryside, the French Riviera, and lots of places in between, but I've never found any place I love as much as my own hometown. Blue skies, gorgeous beaches, the best California sunshine and fresh fruit all year round—it's the kind of place most people only get to read about.

But being able to go to the beach on Christmas Day isn't what makes Sweet Valley so special. It's the people. Not that I haven't met wonderful, interesting people from all parts of the world and all backgrounds. . . . (I even shared a room with an English princess, once.) But it's the people in Sweet Valley who mean the most to me. Let's face it: Growing up is hard, and we all need close friends and family to help us get through the rough patches. So when you ask me, what do those two words—Sweet Valley—mean to me, I have to give a simple answer. My friends and my family.

Speaking of family, I really have a great one. My dad, Ned, is a lawyer, and my mom, Alice, is an interior designer (which is like being an architect, only for the inside of a building). They both have demanding careers, but they never let work get in the way of spending time with us kids—OK, almost never.

My older brother, Steven, is studying to be a lawyer like my dad. My dad won't admit that he would have been disappointed if Steven had decided not to go into law, but if you'd seen the way he was beaming when Steven told him the news . . . well, you'd know he wasn't being quite honest. I can't talk about Steven without mentioning his girlfriend, Billie. She's like a sister to Jessica and me, and she really knows how to keep Steven in line. I hope they get married someday. . . .

No description of my family would be complete without a few thousand pages about my twin sister, Jessica. On the outside we're identical. I guess we're typical California girls—sun-bleached blond hair, blue-green eyes, and slim, athletic figures. We even have the same dimple in our left cheeks. But when you look past our outsides, Jessica and I are opposites!

While I'm curled up in a cozy chair on Sunday afternoon, reading one of my favorite books, like Jane Eyre or Wuthering Heights, Jessica's at the mall, spending money she doesn't have on the most outrageous outfit she can find—preferably made of lycra, and so short it's practically illegal. And when Jessica's off dancing with a dozen gorgeous guys, you can probably find me sitting at a table, having a romantic conversation with my steady boyfriend.

I have a lot of fun, but I take life seriously. (Jessica would probably say too seriously.) I work hard and I always set long-term goals for myself. As a poet, I like to think of myself as the Pacific Ocean on a calm day—tranquil and steady, always there when you need me.

Jess is more like Hurricane Andrew or Mount Saint Helens. She's wild, unpredictable, exciting, and often disastrous. She shows up anywhere, anytime—and when she does, you can bet she's in the spotlight. I pity anyone who tries to stand in my twin's way once she's made up her mind about something. But having said all that, I need to add that Jessica is probably the most lovable person you'll ever meet!

A lot of you may think that having a twin sister must be the greatest thing in the world. Right? From the minute you're born (actually, it was four minutes for me, since I'm older),

4

you have a built-in best friend. You eat together, play together, go to school together—sometimes you even wear matching outfits. No matter where you go or what you do, you know your other half is out there, always willing to come to your rescue when you need it.

Having a twin is great—most of the time. But I have to admit, there are moments when I wish there were just one of me, especially when Jessica develops some hair-brained scheme that involves pretending she's me. And that's probably her greatest talent. For as long as I can remember, Jess has wanted to be a famous actress. Judging by how well she plays the role of Elizabeth Wakefield, I'd wager my computer that she'll win a roomful of Oscars before she has her first gray hair!

In fact, Jessica's desire to be an actress is what inspired her first great twin switch when we were in second grade at Sweet Valley Elementary School. You see, being a twin means you can do a lot of things that regular sisters can't. And at the top of that list is one of Jessica's favorite activities: twin switching. Needless to say, twin switching is when one of us pretends to be the other in order to accomplish something that would otherwise be impossible. Sometimes being each other works out OK, but other times it leads to mayhem—especially when one of us (usually me) doesn't know what the other (usually Jessica) has planned. Maybe if I tell you about a few of our most famous twin switches, you'll see exactly what I'm talking about.

I guess it all started the day I stayed home sick from school, and Jessica decided it would be fun to be me for the day. . . .

Jessica walked into her second-grade classroom and looked around. The first person she saw was her best friend after Elizabeth, Lila Fowler. She wanted to say hello, but she remembered that she was playing Elizabeth that day. She knew that *Elizabeth* thought Lila was stuck-up and would never go talk to Lila. So instead Jessica walked across the room to the hamster cage, where Amy Sutton, Elizabeth's best friend after Jessica, was standing.

"Hi, Amy," Jessica said.

Amy looked up. She opened her mouth to say something, and then stopped. "Hi. Elizabeth?"

"Can't you tell us apart?" Jessica teased. "You know I'm Elizabeth."

6

Amy quickly glanced down at Jessica's wrist to check the name bracelet. It wasn't there because Jessica had left it on her dresser. Amy shrugged.

"Sometimes I forget how much you and Jessica look alike. I almost thought you were Jessica."

"Nope," Jessica said cheerfully.

"Take your seats, everyone," their teacher, Mrs. Otis, said when the bell rang. Jessica sat down in her usual seat, but then popped up again. If she was going to pretend to be Elizabeth, she would have to sit in Elizabeth's chair! She moved over one seat.

"Psst," came a voice from behind her. "Elizabeth."

Jessica turned around. Todd Wilkins was sitting behind her and one seat over.

"I need to tell you something at recess," Todd whispered. "It's a secret. Meet me at the seesaws, OK?"

Jessica smiled. "OK."

When class was over, Jessica hurried to the seesaws and waited for Todd to arrive.

"Let's go over there," Todd whispered, pointing to a tree. "I don't want anyone else to hear."

When they were alone, Todd looked around once more to be sure the coast was clear. Then he said, "A man my parents know is making an afternoon special for TV. He's going to use our house for one part of the movie!"

"Really?" Jessica gasped.

"Plus," Todd went on happily, "I get to be in it."

"Really?" Jessica said even louder. "I wish I could—"

"Shh!" Todd said. "Not so loud." Then he went on. "Plus they need a girl in the scene, so I get to ask one girl I know to be in it. I wanted to ask you first, Elizabeth."

Jessica stared at Todd. She wanted to be in a television movie more than anything in the world, but he wasn't asking *her.*

"Um . . ." she began. "I think Jessica would love to be on TV. She would really, really, really want to do it."

"I don't want to ask Jessica," Todd said. "You know how she is."

"What do you mean?" Jessica asked, trying not to sound angry.

"Nothing," Todd said. "It's just that I want you to be in it."

Jessica looked down at the ground. It

made her feel sad to think that Todd didn't want her. Still, she had to continue pretending she was Elizabeth, or Todd would be really angry at her. "Can Jessica be in it, too?" she asked.

Todd shook his head. "No. And you have to promise not to tell her—not to tell anyone. My mom and dad don't want everybody at school coming over and getting in the way."

"Oh." Jessica folded her arms and tried to think fast.

"You have to come over after school tomorrow," Todd went on. "That's when we're going to rehearse. They call it the run-through. And then we do it for real the day after that."

"OK," Jessica answered slowly. She bit her lip. Maybe if she didn't tell Elizabeth, she could go to Todd's house and keep pretending. That way she'd be in the TV movie.

"Remember, don't tell anyone, Elizabeth," Todd said.

Jessica nodded. She wasn't going to tell a single person.

Elizabeth felt fine the next morning, and Mrs. Wakefield let her go to school.

During attendance, Todd tapped Elizabeth on the shoulder. "Psst," he said.

Elizabeth turned around. Todd was one of the friends she had missed when she was absent. "Hi."

"Don't forget about you know what," he whispered. Todd made his eyes very wide.

Elizabeth blinked in surprise. "What?" she asked.

"Shh!" Todd moved his eyes to the left and the right to remind her there were other people around.

"This afternoon," he said softly. "Don't forget. I'll see you after school, right?"

Next to Elizabeth, Jessica began to cough loudly and move around in her chair.

Elizabeth looked at Jessica. Then she stared at Todd. *He's acting strange*, she thought. They had soccer-league practice after school, but Todd made it seem like a big mystery.

"Yes," Elizabeth whispered back. "I'll see you there." She turned around to face the blackboard again. Then she glanced at Jessica. Her sister was staring straight ahead, and her cheeks were pink. She looked as if she was trying not to cough.

Elizabeth shook her head and took out

her notebook. People sure were acting strange today!

As soon as Jessica got home from school, she changed into jeans and a green T-shirt, one of Elizabeth's favorite outfits.

Jessica got on her bike and rode over to the Wilkinses' house. There were cars and vans parked up and down the street, and people kept going in and out the front door. Jessica walked right in.

"Elizabeth! I'm glad you're here!" Mrs. Wilkins called out as she waved to Jessica from the living room.

Jessica's eyes were round with excitement. All of the people moving furniture and hurrying back and forth with lights were part of the television crew. It was very exciting.

"Hi," Todd said. He looked nervous.

"Hi," Jessica said to Todd. She couldn't stop staring at everything.

"That's Mr. Phillips, the director," Todd said, pointing to a short man in jeans and an old sweatshirt.

Jessica made a face. "Are you sure? He doesn't look very important."

"Positive," Todd said.

"OK, folks," Mr. Phillips said. "Let's do a run-through. Where are the kids?"

"Here!" Jessica yelled, rushing forward. "What do I do?" she asked.

Mr. Phillips came over and put his hands on Jessica's shoulders. "You and Todd will be sitting on the floor, watching TV. Then the phone will ring," he said, pointing to a white telephone.

"That's not our real phone," Todd said.

"Right," the director said. "It's called a prop. When that phone rings, I want Todd to answer it and say 'Lewis residence. Mickey speaking.' Got that?"

"What do I do?" Jessica asked before Todd could answer.

"You keep watching TV," Mr. Phillips said.

Jessica was disappointed. It didn't sound like half as much fun as what Todd was going to do.

"Let's try it," Mr. Phillips said.

A woman turned on the television set and then showed Jessica and Todd where to sit. Jessica sat down and looked at the TV.

"Just relax, Elizabeth," Mr. Phillips told her.

The telephone rang. Jessica jumped up at the same time that Todd did, and they both grabbed the phone.

"Not you!" Todd whispered while they each tried to grab the receiver.

"We're letting Todd answer the phone, Elizabeth," Mr. Phillips reminded her.

"Sorry, I forgot," Jessica said. Pouting, Jessica sat down.

Todd sat down next to her again. "You're acting just like Jessica," he whispered.

"What do you mean?" Jessica asked in a shocked voice.

Todd made a face. "You know. Bossy." Jessica's feelings were hurt, and she started to feel angry at Todd for saying something mean about her. She moved away from him and pretended he wasn't there.

"OK. Let's try it again," the director said.

Jessica raised her hand. "Could we try it once with me answering the phone?"

"You're going to say, 'Mickey speaking'?" Todd said with a laugh.

Jessica stuck her tongue out at him. "Let's just try it the way we planned it, Elizabeth," Mr. Phillips said patiently. Are you ready?"

13

Jessica didn't know whether to be angry or excited. Even if she didn't get to answer the phone, she was still in a TV movie!

Every time she remembered Todd saying that she was bossy, she felt sad and angry all over again. Pretending to be Elizabeth was fun, but she didn't like what she was learning about Jessica!

The next morning, Elizabeth and Jessica walked to the bus stop together. Todd was already there, talking to a group of boys.

"Todd never went to soccer practice yesterday," Elizabeth said to Jessica. It seemed strange to her that he hadn't been there since he had told her that he would see her after school. "I wonder why."

Jessica kicked a pebble. "I don't know."

"Hey, Todd," Elizabeth said, marching up to the group of boys. "What were you going to tell me yesterday afternoon?"

Todd's eyes widened. "Not here!" he whispered.

"Why?" Elizabeth asked in astonishment.

Todd stared at her. "Look at all the people around," he whispered angrily.

"People?" Elizabeth repeated. She was

14

so confused that she didn't know what to say. She was beginning to feel a little angry at Todd for the way he was acting. First he wanted to talk, then he didn't want to talk. It didn't make sense. Elizabeth turned around and walked away.

"I'm angry at Todd," Elizabeth told her sister.

Jessica nodded. "Me, too."

"Why?" Elizabeth asked in surprise. "Why are *you* angry at Todd?"

"Umm . . ." Jessica looked around. "Because you are, that's why. Here comes the bus," she said as she quickly ran to get on.

Elizabeth looked at Jessica. Todd wasn't the only person around who was acting mixed up, she decided.

Elizabeth and Jessica had their usual snack when they got home from school. Elizabeth poured two glasses of milk while Jessica took out some cookies.

"Remember how I said I was angry at Todd?" Elizabeth said.

Jessica stopped with a cookie halfway to her mouth. "Yes?" she said slowly.

"Every time I tried to talk to him today, he started acting strange," Elizabeth went on. She shook her head. "He kept saying stuff like, 'Not here! Not now!' I think I'm going to go over to his house and ask him what's going on."

"NO!" Jessica yelled.

Elizabeth looked at her. "Why not?"

"Because . . ." Jessica wriggled in her chair. "I . . . I heard him say he had a dentist appointment. And then, I think his grandmother is coming over." Jessica bit into her cookie and didn't say anything else. Her cheeks were pink.

"Oh." Elizabeth took a sip of milk. "I'll wait until tomorrow, then." She stood up and went to the door. "I'm going to do my homework and then read my new book."

When Elizabeth was all done, she looked out the window. It was such a nice, sunny afternoon that she thought it would be fun to play outside instead of reading. She closed her notebook and ran downstairs. "Mom?" she called out.

Mrs. Wakefield was in the living room. "Yes, Jessica?"

"Mom!" Elizabeth laughed, sitting down next to her.

"Oh, Elizabeth." Mrs. Wakefield made a

face and smiled. "I thought you went out with Steven a while ago."

Elizabeth shook her head. "I was doing homework."

"That's funny," Mrs. Wakefield said. "I guess it was Jessica, then. Steven said he was walking her over to Todd's house to play basketball. He'll be back any minute."

"Todd's house?" Elizabeth repeated. "Basketball?"

"I could have sworn he'd said, 'Come on, Liz.' But it must have been Jessica," Mrs. Wakefield said. "We can ask him when he returns."

Elizabeth felt angry. Hadn't Jessica said that Todd wouldn't be home? Elizabeth was so upset, she didn't know what to think. But she was going to find out.

Elizabeth went outside, picked up her bike, and pedaled slowly to Todd's house. She saw vans and cars blocking the street. There seemed to be a crowd of people, too. It looked like they were all right in front of the Wilkinses' house.

"Is there a big party?" Elizabeth wondered out loud.

She rode a little closer. She could see electrical wire running from the trucks right inside the Wilkinses' front door. The inside of the house looked filled with people. *Jessica must be there, too,* Elizabeth thought.

What is going on? she wondered.

"Where's Elizabeth," Mr. Phillips asked. "What are all these kids doing here?"

Jessica squeezed her eyes shut. Even though she'd promised Todd that she would keep today a secret, she hadn't been able to resist telling Lila and Ellen Riteman. Either Lila or Ellen had invited all these people. Jessica knew it was her fault, though. What a mess she had gotten herself into.

Elizabeth leaned her bike on its kickstand and looked around. People were running back and forth, carrying big electrical cables as well as lighting and camera equipment. She could see almost all the kids in Mrs. Otis's second-grade class.

"What's going on?" Elizabeth asked Caroline.

"Movie stars!" Caroline said in a hushed voice. "There are movie stars coming."

Elizabeth looked at the house in surprise. "Movie stars?" She walked a few steps closer, and Todd came running out of the house. He saw Elizabeth and rushed over to her.

"Elizabeth!" he yelled, sounding angry.

"What is going on?" Elizabeth asked, walking toward him.

Todd glared at her. "I told you not to tell anybody! My mom and dad are really mad at me, and I'm really mad at you! Mr. Phillips is angry at everybody." He turned around and stomped away.

"Wait a second!" Elizabeth said. She ran after Todd. "I don't know what you're talking about!"

Todd made a face. "Oh, sure. You didn't tell anyone at school?"

"Tell them *what*?" Elizabeth held her hands up and shook her head. "I didn't tell anybody anything because I don't know what I wasn't supposed to tell!"

"But—" Todd stopped talking and stared at her. He looked upset. "But you were right here with me and Mr. Phillips yesterday when we did the run-through and everything."

Elizabeth stared at Todd and shook her head. "Todd, I don't—" Suddenly she put one hand over her mouth and gasped. She had the answer.

Todd's mouth dropped open. He started shaking his head from side to side. "It wasn't you yesterday, was it? When I told you in school on Tuesday—"

"I was *absent* on Tuesday," Elizabeth said.

"Oh, no," Todd said. "Wait till I find Jessica! I thought she was you, and I wanted you to be in the movie with me, and she came over yesterday—"

"I was at soccer practice yesterday," Elizabeth said. "She didn't want me to come over to your house today, and she's already here—somewhere."

"She's going to get in trouble," Todd said.

They both charged in through the front door, shouting the same thing.

"*Jessica!*"

Jessica thought it was just about time to go downstairs and see what was happening. She began to tiptoe down the steps. "Jessica!" yelled two voices at once. Jessica froze. Staring up at her from the bottom of the staircase were Elizabeth and Todd. They both looked angry! "Umm . . ." she said.

20

"What's the big idea?" Elizabeth started to say. But before she could go on, Mr. Phillips came into the hallway from the living room. He took Elizabeth and Todd by the hand.

"Come on, kids! Let's get moving here. We're all set up and ready," he said.

"Mr. Phillips, wait," Todd said.

Mr. Phillips looked up and noticed Jessica standing at the top of the stairs. Jessica gave him an apologetic smile and waved one hand. The director blinked in surprise and looked at Elizabeth again.

"Twins?" he said. He let out a laugh. "Well, what do you know! Which one of you is Elizabeth?"

"I am," Elizabeth said. "But I think Jessica is the one you know."

"Hold on a minute, kids!" the director said. "Who was here yesterday?"

"Me," Jessica said, raising her hand.

"And you're not Elizabeth?" Mr. Phillips asked.

Jessica shook her head.

"Well, this is getting complicated," Mr. Phillips said with a laugh. "I guess I'll use all three of you."

Elizabeth turned around and stared at

him. "But . . ."

"Come on, Liz," Jessica said as she ran down the stairs and took Elizabeth's hand. "Let's do what he says!"

"But . . ." Elizabeth began.

Jessica knew her sister was very angry at her. But everyone was suddenly in a hurry, and there wasn't any time to say anything. They all followed the director into the living room.

"Look at this, everyone!" Mr. Phillips said. "We've got twins! A nice touch, I think." He turned to the twins.

"Now, Elizabeth," Mr. Phillips said. "Remember what we did yesterday?"

"No, I wasn't—" Elizabeth began.

"Right!" The director slapped one hand to his forehead. "OK! From the top. Kids, sit down in front of the television."

Elizabeth, Todd, and Jessica sat down.

"When the phone rings, Todd is going to answer it," Jessica whispered to Elizabeth.

"How do you know the phone is going to ring?" Elizabeth whispered back.

Jessica giggled. "It's a fake phone. Watch." Mr. Phillips stood behind a big movie camera to see how they looked. "OK. We're rolling."

Jessica's heart was beating loudly in her

chest. She watched the television and tried not to notice all the people around her. Suddenly the telephone rang.

"Lewis residence. Mickey speaking," Todd said when he picked it up.

"And, cut!" Mr. Phillips said. "Perfect, Todd. You did a great job. Now let's try it again. This time, I'd like Elizabeth . . ."

"Which Elizabeth?" Jessica interrupted. Mr. Phillips grinned. "The real one, please. Let's have Elizabeth and Todd fight over who gets to answer the phone. The way you did yesterday."

"But—" Jessica said. Her big smile disappeared. It looked like Elizabeth was going to get a bigger part in the scene, and all because Jessica had tried grabbing the phone in the run-through!

"OK," Elizabeth said.

"Places, everyone. And . . . action!" Mr. Phillips pointed to them.

The three kids watched the television, and when the phone rang, Elizabeth and Todd both jumped up to answer it. Todd grabbed it away first and said his line.

"Lewis residence. Mickey speaking."

"And cut!" Mr. Phillips shouted. "Perfect! That's a wrap!"

*　　*　　*

"Come on," Elizabeth said to Jessica.

"We want to talk to you." When the twins and Todd got outside, Jessica looked from Elizabeth to Todd and back again. "You aren't mad at me, are you?"

"I am!" Todd said. "You were pretending to be Elizabeth the whole time. Then you told my secret to everyone."

"I'm mad at you, too!" Elizabeth said. "You knew Todd wanted me to be in the movie and you weren't going to tell me!"

Jessica gulped. "But, well, I'm mad at you!" she said to Todd. "You said mean things about me!"

"I didn't say them to you," Todd said. He looked embarrassed.

Elizabeth frowned. "What mean things did you say about Jessica?" she asked. She didn't like anyone to criticize her sister.

"He said I was acting bossy!" Jessica said. "That's mean!"

"It is, but it's sort of true sometimes," Elizabeth said. "How come you pretended to be me when I was absent from school?" Elizabeth asked. She still felt hurt that Jessica would do that.

"It was only a joke," Jessica said honestly.

24

"You and I like to pretend we're each other. And when I left my name bracelet at home, people thought I was you. I only meant it as a game. And then, and then . . . I couldn't stop. I didn't think it would cause so much trouble. I'm sorry, Liz," Jessica said.

"I forgive you," Elizabeth said, rubbing her sneaker on the ground. "Besides, I think you learned your lesson."

Elizabeth smiled. *Jessica will always be Jessica,* she decided. And she would always be Elizabeth. They could never, ever really be each other, because they were so different.

So that's how Jessica almost stole my first chance at being on television. I must admit, though, it was more fun being in the TV movie with Jess than it would have been alone! In fact, almost everything I do is more fun when Jessica's there to share it with me. I guess that's the best part about being a twin—there's always someone to share with!

I don't want Jessica to accuse me of being a Goody Two-shoes, so I'd better explain that she's not the only one who's capable of doing a secret twin switch. There was one time in sixth grade . . .

PART TWO

Hi! I'm Jessica Wakefield, and Liz is crazy if she thinks she's the authority on what it's like to be a twin. I mean, if I let her do all the explaining, you'd think she was Saint Elizabeth and I was Jessica the Terrible. There are two sides to every story, and I intend to tell my side!

First of all, Elizabeth described us as "typical California girls." That might be true for Liz, but Jessica Wakefield is anything but typical. Take our hair, for example. She says it's bleached blond by the sun. How boring can you get? I'll have you know that our hair is soft, silky, and—my favorite description—sun-kissed. Our eyes aren't just blue-green, either. They happen to be the exact color of the Pacific Ocean! Are you getting my drift?

26

Anyway, Elizabeth was right about me thinking she takes life too seriously. If it were up to her, she'd probably be chained to her computer, books, and boyfriend. Luckily, I have great powers of persuasion. I manage to get her away from her desk and out into the sun pretty often. She might not say so, but Liz knows that without me her life would be completely and totally dull!

As the impulsive, spontaneous, exciting twin, I guess I have to confess that Elizabeth's boring, sensible nature has gotten me out of some pretty major scrapes in my life. And as much as I hate to say it, Liz does have an annoying habit of knowing what's best for me. Sometimes. Well . . . usually.

But if you really want to understand Elizabeth, you can't be fooled by her all-I-care-about-is-writing-and-saving-the-world routine. Elizabeth has just as many faults as the rest of us. She's just better at hiding them!

Take twin switching. Elizabeth is a master at that game!

I'll never forget our first Valentine's Day dance back in sixth grade. We expected the night to be perfect! But instead of the romantic evening of our lives, Liz and I ended up in a huge fight with each other—Todd Wilkins ditched her for awful Veronica Brooks, I ditched Aaron Dallas for snobby Bruce Patman, and worst of all, Aaron and Liz ended up together! The whole next week was miserable, especially because we both missed our sort-of boyfriends.

So when Ellen Riteman decided to have a party, Liz and I both had the idea that we would not only make up with each other, we'd also surprise each other by getting back together with our boyfriends.

It was an eventful night, to say the least. . . .

Elizabeth paced around her room. *Why does Jessica always have to take so long to get ready?* she thought impatiently. *How am I supposed to copy what she's wearing if she won't hurry up and get dressed? I'll sneak through the bathroom and take another look.*

She carefully opened the door to the bathroom. Then she slowly stepped inside— and found herself face-to-face with Jessica!

"Aren't you dressed yet?" Jessica exclaimed, glaring at Elizabeth. Elizabeth tried frantically to think of another excuse. "I was just . . ." Elizabeth glanced around the bathroom and noticed her denim skirt hanging on a hook. ". . . looking for my denim skirt," she finished. "There it is."

"You're wearing that?" Jessica asked eagerly.

Elizabeth sighed. She was stuck now. "Yes," she answered.

Jessica bit her lip. "You know, I was thinking of wearing my denim miniskirt, too."

"Oh, really?" Elizabeth said. This was good news.

"If we wear different tops, it won't make any difference, right?" Jessica said.

"Right," Elizabeth agreed encouragingly.

"Good," Jessica said. She turned and hurried out of the bathroom.

It's about time, Jessica thought as she rummaged through her closet in search of her own denim miniskirt. Things were going to be tricky, but she was pretty sure she could pull it off.

For once she didn't spend much time getting ready. She pulled a plain blue blouse out of her closet and decided not to curl her hair. She didn't really want people to pay much attention to her that night.

She heard the door to Elizabeth's room open. "Ready?" Jessica asked, noting Elizabeth's pink sweater.

"Ready," Elizabeth said.

"I'll be right there." Jessica shut her door quickly and hurried to her closet. She had a pink sweater almost exactly like the one Elizabeth was wearing. When she found it, she stuffed it down into the bottom of her large purse.

She rushed back out to the hall, but Elizabeth was gone. Jessica figured that she must already have gone downstairs. But just then the door to Elizabeth's room opened and she came out. "Let's party," she said with a grin.

Jessica was startled. *Wow, Elizabeth sounds just like me.*

Ellen Riteman's party was in full swing, and Jessica decided it was time to ditch Bruce and put her plan in motion. Jessica threw one last look over her shoulder to make sure that Bruce hadn't noticed her disappearance. Then she grabbed her purse and hurried toward the bathroom in the laundry room off the kitchen.

She slipped inside and locked the door behind her. It didn't take her long to change out of her blue blouse and into the pink sweater. As she combed her hair into a ponytail, she forced her face into a serious and shy expression. "Hi, Todd," she said softly, doing her best to imitate her sister.

Come on! Elizabeth thought impatiently. She had been standing outside the downstairs bathroom for five minutes. Whoever was in there was sure taking a long time. Elizabeth was afraid Aaron would come looking for her if she didn't get back out to the patio soon. It hadn't been easy to get away. Aaron was a real party animal.

I'd better find another bathroom upstairs, Elizabeth decided. She hurried up the stairs and found one on the upstairs landing. She ducked inside and fished a plain blue blouse out of her purse.

In less than two minutes she had completed her transformation. She tossed her head and tried out a flirtatious look in the mirror. "Hi, Aaron," she said with a big smile, doing her best to look and sound like Jessica. Then she took a deep breath, opened the bathroom door, and headed off to find Aaron.

"Hi, Todd. Having a good time?"

When Todd looked up and saw someone

he thought was Elizabeth standing next to him, he jumped in surprise and almost choked on the mint he was eating.

He began to cough and Jessica pounded him on the back. "Sorry if I scared you," she said in Elizabeth's sweetest voice.

Todd managed to catch his breath. "You didn't *scare* me." He took a big gulp of soda. "You just surprised me. I mean, I thought you weren't speaking to me."

"I wasn't," Jessica said. "But then I realized I was being really silly. We're old friends, right?"

"Sure," Todd said, doing his best to look cool and unconcerned. He leaned back casually against the wall, but it was farther away than he realized. "Whoa!" he cried as he began to fall.

Quick as lightning, Jessica reached out and caught Todd by the lapels of his shirt. "Watch it," she said, briskly hoisting him to his feet.

Todd's face was beet red. He hastily brushed himself off. "Uh . . . thanks," he stammered. "I don't know what happened there. I just sort of lost my balance for a minute."

Jessica smiled inwardly. There was no

longer any doubt in her mind that Todd still liked Elizabeth. How else could a person possibly be so nervous and klutzy?

"It could happen to anyone," Jessica said, trying to make her voice sound really understanding. "In fact, it's even happened to me once or twice." Jessica did her best to giggle like Elizabeth as she patted the collar of Todd's shirt back into shape. "So, Todd . . ." she said.

Todd looked at her gravely. Jessica knew this was going to be tough. He was pretty intelligent. And so was Elizabeth. Jessica bit her lip. She needed to think of something intelligent to talk about.

"So, Todd," she began again, "read any good books lately?"

"Hi, Aaron," Elizabeth said, giving Aaron a dazzling smile.

Aaron automatically smiled back. "Hi," he said happily. Then his face clouded over as he remembered that he and Jessica weren't speaking. "See you later," he mumbled, turning to walk away.

Normally, Elizabeth would have been humiliated by such a pointed rejection.

You're not Elizabeth, she reminded herself. *You're Jessica. Be more aggressive.*

"Don't run away," she said quickly. "I was hoping maybe we could dance."

Aaron frowned. "Elizabeth is my date," he reminded her. "And Bruce Patman is yours," he added angrily. "Last time you dumped me to dance with Bruce. This time you're dumping Bruce to dance with me. What are you trying to do, anyway? Be the date-dumping champion of Sweet Valley?"

Aaron sounded really angry. But Elizabeth knew he was angry because his feelings were hurt.

Elizabeth loved and admired Jessica. But she was glad that it was she and not her sister who was having this conversation with Aaron. Jessica wasn't always as perceptive as Elizabeth. She might not have realized that Aaron's anger came from hurt feelings. Her response would probably be to get angry herself. Then she would say something even more hurtful, and the situation would get worse.

Jessica may have more spunk than I do, thought Elizabeth. *But I have more tact. And this is definitely a situation that calls for tact.*

"Gosh, Aaron," Elizabeth said, "I'm

34

sorry you think that. I wasn't trying to do anything that would hurt your feelings. I saw you over here by yourself and thought it would be a good opportunity for us to talk—and maybe be friends again."

Aaron looked ashamed. "I'm sorry," he muttered. "I guess I sounded a little harsh."

"That's OK," Elizabeth assured him. "I don't blame you. The last few days have been kind of rough."

"What do you mean, rough?" he asked quickly. "Rough on who? Not me. Elizabeth is a great girl. I really like being with her. So don't say anything bad about her."

"Of course Elizabeth is a great girl," Elizabeth said. "And because she's so great, she wants you to be happy. She's a great sister, too. And that means she wants me to be happy."

"Uh-huh." Aaron frowned with the effort of trying to follow her reasoning. "So?"

"Are you happy, Aaron?" Elizabeth asked, looking soulfully into his eyes.

"Sure. I guess so. Why not? I mean, I hadn't really thought about it." He stared back at her. "But now that you ask, maybe I'm not as happy as I used to be," he admitted softly.

"I'm not as happy as I used to be, either," Elizabeth said bluntly.

"Really?" Aaron stared at her warily. He still didn't seem completely sure whether or not to trust her. "Why not?" he asked suspiciously.

Elizabeth touched his arm. "Probably for the same reason you're not happy. And I don't think Elizabeth is happy, either."

"You don't?" Aaron asked.

Elizabeth shook her head. "No. That's probably why she did so poorly on her math homework."

Aaron shook his head sadly. "Yeah, I sort of wondered about that myself. You think it's because of me, huh? Because she doesn't really like me?"

"It's not that I—that she doesn't like you," Elizabeth said. *Careful*, she told herself. "It's probably because she still likes Todd. Just like I still like you," she added boldly.

"Wow," Aaron said. He gave a low whistle. "You still like me? This is really sort of a big mess, isn't it?"

There was a burst of laughter from the other side of the room, and they both looked over to see Bruce surrounded by adoring Unicorns. The sight seemed to remind Aaron of what had started the big mess.

He scowled at Jessica. "If you like me so much, how come you left me standing all alone at the dance and went off with Bruce?"

Good question, Elizabeth thought. But she was prepared for it. "You know how carried away I get with things. Being asked to dance by a seventh-grader is every sixth-grade girl's dream. If some girl in the seventh grade paid a lot of attention to you, wouldn't it turn *your* head?"

Aaron looked thoughtful. "Yeah, I guess it would. So I suppose I can't really blame you." He scowled again. "But did you have to kiss him?"

Elizabeth sighed. "Let me see if I can explain about that."

"So anyway," Todd said, "the best part of the book was the ending, where the count gets his revenge and . . ."

Jessica smiled and opened her eyes very wide, trying to look interested. She tightened her jaw to stifle another yawn. Todd had just told her the entire plot of the book he had just read. It was a very long and complicated story, and Jessica was starting to feel a little sleepy.

Was this really the kind of stuff Todd and Elizabeth talked about? How incredibly boring! Maybe she wasn't doing Elizabeth such a big favor by getting her back together with Todd.

"It was really exciting," Todd went on. "It was almost as good as the other book I read last week."

"The *other* book?" Jessica said, stunned. "You read *two* books last week? For fun?" *Get a life,* she thought. Then she remembered that she was supposed to be Elizabeth. "I mean, that's great," she said. "I can't believe you read two whole books."

As soon as it was out of her mouth, she knew it was the wrong thing to say.

"What's the big deal?" Todd asked impatiently. "You read at least two books almost every week." Then a disgusted look crossed his face and he rolled his eyes. "Oh, I get it. You're doing the kind of stuff Jessica does. Pretending to be really impressed with a guy to build up his ego and make him like you."

"Jessica doesn't do that kind of thing," Jessica retorted.

Todd looked skeptical. "Yes, she does. Rick Hunter told me all about it."

Jessica began to blush furiously. Actually, she knew that she sometimes *did* do that kind of thing. But it was pretty embarrassing to realize that Rick Hunter was making fun of her for doing it.

"OK," she admitted grudgingly. "Maybe she does, just a little. But Eliz—but I don't," she corrected herself quickly.

She was beginning to get a little rattled. The twins had changed places lots of times, but this was the first time Jessica had tried to fool a boyfriend. It was more nerve-wracking than she had expected.

She smiled weakly. "I'm just so glad to hear that you still like to read," she explained. "I thought you might have changed. But you haven't," she babbled nervously. "You still love to read. I love to read. We both love to read. That's why we have so much in common. And since we do have all this stuff in common, I really think we should be friends again."

Jessica batted her eyelashes—just a little. "Don't you think we should be friends again?" she continued in a coaxing tone. It wasn't really Elizabeth's style, but Jessica just couldn't help herself. Besides, she figured it wouldn't hurt Elizabeth to try a little eyelash-batting once in a while.

Todd snorted and batted his eyelashes back at her. "I *used* to think so. Now I'm not so sure." He looked at his watch. "Geez, I've spent almost ten minutes yakking about books."

Only ten minutes? Jessica thought in amazement. It had seemed more like an hour to her.

"I'd better find my date," Todd said. "I don't want to be rude." He started to walk away, but Jessica grabbed his sleeve and yanked him back.

"Veronica's busy talking to Bruce," she said. "Don't worry about her."

Todd looked startled at Elizabeth's sudden aggressiveness. "You're the one who's changed, Elizabeth," he suddenly burst out. "And not for the better, either."

"How have I changed?" Jessica demanded.

"Veronica told me what you did," he said. "At first I had a lot of trouble believing you would do something like that, but—"

"What did I do?"

"Hey," said a sharp voice behind Jessica. "Why don't you quit bothering my date?"

Jessica whirled around and saw Veronica giving her a dirty look. Jessica put her hands on her hips. "Do you mind? We're trying to have a private conversation here."

"As a matter of fact," Veronica purred, "I do mind. Todd is my date." She took Todd's arm and looked at him. "And I'd like to dance now."

"Why don't you dance with Bruce Patman?" Jessica sneered. "You sure seemed to think he was fascinating a few minutes ago."

Todd gasped. "Elizabeth! Don't talk to Veronica that way."

Jessica's heart sank. Elizabeth would never behave this way. Jessica was afraid she had just blown things permanently between Todd and her sister. This whole scheme had been a terrible mistake.

"Pssst! Pssst!" an insistent voice hissed behind her.

Jessica turned and saw Amy frantically waving at her from the other side of the

41

patio. She shook her head. Sometimes Amy Sutton was so weird. She was going to have to speak to Elizabeth about her. That made Jessica remember that she was supposed to *be* Elizabeth. "Excuse me," she said as politely as she could. "I'll be right back."

She hurried over to Amy. "What is it? I'm a little busy right now."

"I'm trying to stop you before you make a fool of yourself," Amy said urgently. "Todd really likes Veronica. No kidding. He gave her a locket just like the one he gave you. She's wearing it tonight—I saw it."

"A locket?" Jessica repeated.

Right then something clicked in her head. Elizabeth had asked her about a missing locket earlier that evening. And now, suddenly, Veronica had one. Jessica had been so mad at Elizabeth last week that she'd actually had snobby Veronica over to try to hurt her twin's feelings. Hadn't Veronica slipped something into her pocket while she'd been snooping in Elizabeth's room? It must have been Elizabeth's locket.

Jessica whirled around, fire in her eyes. She was so angry that for a moment she forgot she was supposed to be Elizabeth.

All she knew was that Veronica was the dirtiest trickster she had ever met in her whole life. And this time she wasn't going to get away with it. She stalked back over to Veronica and held out her hand.

"Hand it over," she demanded furiously.

Veronica gave her an innocent look. "What are you talking about?"

"Hand over the locket. The one you stole from Eli—from me!"

"*Stole?*" Todd exclaimed. "What are you talking about?"

Jessica pointed at the locket around Veronica's neck. "That! Veronica stole it from my room!"

Todd turned to Veronica. "You said you found it in the garbage can at school. You said you saw her throw it away after she and I broke up."

"I did," Veronica insisted.

"She did *not*," Jessica fumed. "And while we're on the subject," she said, glaring at Todd, "why is she wearing Eli—my locket?"

Todd flushed.

"Why shouldn't I wear it?" Veronica sneered. "*I'm* Todd's girlfriend now. Besides, you threw the locket away."

"That's not true," Jessica shouted. "You took it the day you were over at my house."

"You're a liar!" Veronica shouted back.

Todd frowned. "I've never known Elizabeth to tell a lie," he said thoughtfully. He gave Veronica a serious look. "Tell me the truth, Veronica. Did you really take it? Were you just trying to make more trouble between me and Elizabeth?"

"She *was* trying to make trouble," Jessica said.

Veronica shoved Jessica's shoulder. "Why don't you get lost and let me and Todd work this out?"

Jessica shoved Veronica back. "What makes you such a jerk, anyway?"

Veronica shoved Jessica again, a little harder. "What makes you such a goody-goody?"

"Who are you calling a goody-goody?" Jessica hissed, pushing Veronica so that she stumbled into Todd.

"Please stop it, Elizabeth," Todd begged.

"Stay out of this," snapped Veronica. She gave Jessica a hard shove that sent her hurtling backward across the patio, through the door, and into the living room.

*   *   *

44

"So you never really wanted to kiss Bruce?"

"No," Elizabeth repeated for the fifteenth time.

"I just couldn't get out of the way fast enough." She knew she was probably stretching the truth a little. But after all, stretching the truth was Jessica's specialty.

Aaron sighed happily. "Oh, Jessica, I can't believe how silly we've—" But he never got to finish his sentence.

There were several surprised shouts and an outraged yelp. The crowd in the living room parted as a figure came careening through the living room as if she had been shot from a cannon.

"Yeow!" cried the figure as she tripped over a stereo speaker and sprawled at Elizabeth's feet.

Elizabeth looked down and blinked in surprise. Jessica stared back up at her, looking equally astonished.

Before either girl could say a word, Todd came rushing into the room. "Elizabeth! Elizabeth!" he cried out. "Are you all right?"

Elizabeth? thought Elizabeth as she watched Todd help her sister to her feet.

"Are you all right, Jessica?" Todd asked,

45

turning to Elizabeth. "It looked like Elizabeth almost fell right on top of you."

"I'm fine," Elizabeth managed to squeak.

As she watched, Todd turned back toward her sister. "I'm so sorry, Elizabeth. I believe you about Veronica. I believe you about the locket. I believe you about everything. And I'm sorry I abandoned you at the dance. Can we please be friends again?"

Aaron turned to Elizabeth. "Can we be friends again, too, Jessica?"

At that moment, a romantic ballad began to play. "Let's make it up with a kiss," sang Johnny Buck over the speakers.

Elizabeth smiled at Aaron. Jessica smiled at Todd.

Aaron grinned back at Elizabeth and leaned forward, preparing to seal the happy moment with a kiss. Todd smiled happily at Jessica and got ready to do the same. But just then, both twins spoke at once. "Excuse me," they said.

They hurried out of the living room. "This way," Jessica said. She grabbed Elizabeth's hand and pulled her toward the bathroom in the laundry room.

Once they were inside, Jessica shut the

door with a bang and both girls began to laugh hysterically.

"I can't believe you," Elizabeth exclaimed breathlessly.

"Look who's talking," Jessica gasped back.

"This proves it," Elizabeth said, unbuttoning the blue blouse and handing it to Jessica. "Great minds think alike."

Luckily, that story had a happy ending, and Liz and I were closer than ever. But if you think that night in sixth grade was devious, you won't believe the stunt she pulled when we spent the summer in London when we were sixteen. Liz was a regular Mata Hari!

I think I'll let Liz explain this one herself. Only she can describe how far she'll go when she's worried I'm in danger—and boy can my twin worry!

PART THREE

As always, Jessica is guilty of exaggerating. According to her, I'd probably jump out of an airplane or hide a camera in my wristwatch if I thought it would help me spoil her plans. In reality, I'd never stand in Jessica's way of a good time unless my sixth sense—I call it my twin radar—detected danger for Jessica. And it's the same for her.

Our whole lives, we've been able to perceive if the other was in grave danger. It's a good thing, too, because over the years we've both been in some scary situations. One time Jessica saved me from being stabbed to death by a psychotic girl named Margo, who had delusions that if she killed me, she could take over my identity!

48

But Jessica's referring to the summer we got internships at the London Journal. Jess and I were both excited to be in London, but for different reasons. I wanted to explore the city and sharpen the journalism skills I'd developed working on the Sweet Valley High newspaper, The Oracle. As usual, Jessica's entire brain was devoted to two concepts: boys and shopping. She insisted I was a loser for wanting to be faithful to my boyfriend, Todd, while she went carousing for wealthy English noblemen.

You may have already guessed that our time in London didn't turn out quite as we had planned! When we arrived, there was a full moon. I'm not normally a superstitious person, but there was something about that glowing yellow moon that made the hairs on the back of my neck stand up. Jessica said I was being ridiculous—for once, she assumed the role of Ms. Practical.

And then there was Luke. I'm ashamed to tell you that despite my vow to stay with Todd, I found myself falling head over heels for a guy who worked at the London Journal. His name was Luke Shepherd, and when I met him he seemed so sensitive and intelligent. He was also as interested as I was in the mysterious, bloody murders that had been taking place in London.

49

We became close—I thought I could trust him with my life.

Jessica wasn't far behind me when it came to falling in love that summer. She met the elite and prestigious Robert Pembroke and decided on the spot that he was the man she was destined to marry. There's no halfway with my twin sister!

To make a long story short, let's just say that I didn't trust the Pembroke family. One weekend Jessica and Luke and I went to Pembroke Manor, and one night another guest, Joy Singleton, was brutally killed, her throat ripped open and chewed on. I knew that Robert's father was using his power to cover up the details of this and the other grisly murders. My twin radar was telling me that Jessica's new boyfriend was not only the culprit but also a werewolf (don't scoff—there was a full moon!). You see, Luke had studied the patterns of werewolves for years, and he was convinced that the murderer was one of those powerfully evil and deadly beasts.

I'd done some investigating the weekend of Joy's murder, but I was convinced that if I went back to Pembroke Manor, I could find solid evidence to condemn Robert Pembroke. Unfortunately, the Pembrokes had witnessed my prior detective work (such as interviewing all of the servants), and I knew they wouldn't be wild about having me around.

As I explained to my London roommate, Eliana, the circumstances left me no choice. I had to go to Pembroke Manor under the guise of being the one and only Jessica Wakefield. . . .

"I plan to travel to Pembroke Manor tomorrow, disguised as Jessica, to see if I can get some information about the newspaper cover-up. I want to know what Pembroke is hiding," Elizabeth said to her roommate, Eliana.

"But, Liz," Eliana asked, "what if Lord Pembroke mentions to Robert that 'Jessica' came to see him, and Robert mentions it to Jess?"

Elizabeth shrugged. "It's worth the risk. When I find absolute proof that something is criminally wrong at Pembroke Manor, Jessica will have to forgive me. And I intend to find proof."

The grandfather clock in the parlor had just chimed nine o'clock when the phone rang on Pembroke's desk, startling him out of a fitful doze.

"Hello, Lord Pembroke!" exclaimed a breathless, youthful voice at the other end of the line.

For the first time in days, a genuine smile sprang to Pembroke's face. The caller could be no one but Robert's young lady friend, Jessica Wakefield.

"I have a few itsy-bitsy questions for you about that mink coat of Lady Pembroke's—for a follow-up article in the newspaper, of course," Jessica said brightly, referring to the story the twins had written about Lady Pembroke's stolen fur. "Would you mind if I dropped by Pembroke Manor this afternoon to talk to you about it?"

"I wouldn't mind at all, child," he told her. "Glad to have you anytime. In fact, you should plan to stay for supper and to spend the night as well. We've plenty of room, and Lord knows we could use some cheer around here!"

Then his eyes narrowed as suspicions rose in his mind. "You will be alone, won't you, dear?" he asked. "That is to say, you don't plan to bring that twin sister of yours, do you?"

"Oh, no," Jessica assured him. "I'm working on this story all by myself."

Thank goodness, he thought as Jessica chatted on about her internship.

It was remarkable that a guileless girl like Jessica could have an identical twin who was so nosy and suspicious, Pembroke thought. Elizabeth was the Wakefield he had to watch out for.

Elizabeth paid the taxi driver and began walking up the long driveway to Pembroke manor through a misty rain. Elizabeth cleared the crest of the hill, and the front of stately Pembroke Manor rose into sight. Elizabeth gasped. Red lights flashed through the rain, from an ambulance that waited in front of the mansion's grand entranceway. Uniformed police officers and medical personnel rushed around the ambulance while servants huddled together on the front portico, watching.

"Jessica," Lord Pembroke said in a distracted voice as he caught sight of Elizabeth. "In all the commotion, I quite forgot you would be arriving. You're welcome to stay, of course. But there's been an unfortunate incident."

"What's happened?" Elizabeth asked.

Instead of answering, Pembroke placed

a hand on her shoulder. Elizabeth was surprised to feel it trembling.

"Jessica," he said. "See that you don't mention today's, er, event to anyone at the newspaper—including that sister of yours. It is the subject of a police investigation, so any publicity at this time would be inappropriate." He spoke quietly, but his voice held a note of thinly disguised panic.

"Oh, you can count on me," Elizabeth assured him. "But I will stay, if you don't mind. Can you tell me what's—"

Before she finished speaking, Pembroke had turned away, satisfied, and was hurrying toward Constable Atherton, who was waiting for him near the ambulance with her arms folded impatiently in front of her.

Elizabeth approached the house and skirted the row of parked police cars. As she neared the clustered servants, she saw that most of them were weeping. "What in the world is going on?" she asked under her breath. "And is it related to the deaths of Joy and the others?"

She quickly decided on a course of action. After she learned what had just happened, she would slip inside the manor house and search for clues about the were-wolf's identity and the Pembrokes' part in the murders.

Two servants passed close to where Elizabeth stood behind a hedge. ". . . found murdered this morning," she heard one of them say.

"Who was found murdered?" Elizabeth asked herself out loud.

A moment later she had her answer. Alistair, the tall, thin butler who had served tea on the morning of Joy's death, was led, sobbing, out of the house. Behind him, two paramedics carried a stretcher bearing what Elizabeth knew was a sheet-covered corpse. The constable lifted the sheet, and Elizabeth gasped.

On the stretcher lay the body of the Pembrokes' pretty, brown-haired cook, Maria Finch. Even from a distance, Elizabeth could see on her throat a bright red gash.

Elizabeth stood in Robert's room at Pembroke Manor on Tuesday afternoon, feeling guilty about prowling around his bedroom. *Maybe I should have just stayed in London*, she thought.

Elizabeth sighed, impatient with her

own indecision. She had been thinking in circles all day—ever since the phone call to Lord Pembroke that morning. Maybe she was totally off base, suspecting them of murder. But then she remembered the odd way Lord Pembroke had ended their telephone conversation.

"I want you to know that Robert loves you very much," he had said. *"Please remember that—no matter what happens."*

No matter what happens? "What does that mean?" she asked herself aloud for the tenth time that day. "Does it mean that Lord Pembroke is protecting his son? Is young Robert Pembroke a serial murderer—and a werewolf?"

She felt a prickling along her spine and was grateful that Jessica was not planning to see Robert that day. *And after today I might have enough evidence to keep her from seeing him ever again.*

The scene that had taken place in front of the mansion a half hour earlier played back in Elizabeth's mind. The recollection of the cook's body helped Elizabeth steel herself for prying into Robert's belongings. She had to know, beyond any doubt, if he had killed Maria and the other victims.

As Elizabeth prepared to search the room for clues, the question she had tried to banish from her mind suddenly shoved its way to the forefront. Was Maria dead because of Elizabeth's investigation? Had somebody discovered that the servants had spoken to her?

She shook her head. "I won't think about that right now," she whispered. "The most important thing now is to prove who the murderer is. If it's Robert Pembroke, something in this room ought to tell me that."

She started poking around Robert's spacious bedroom, unsure of exactly what she was searching for. But when she opened the door to the enormous walk-in closet, Elizabeth gasped. She finally had her proof.

Hanging inside the closet door was a paisley-patterned silk bathrobe in hunter green—with a small tear on one shoulder.

With trembling hands, Elizabeth removed the envelope from her backpack and pulled out the threads she had taken from the doorway at the murder scene. The bathrobe was a perfect match. Robert Pembroke had been in the room where Joy Singleton was murdered!

Elizabeth jumped at the sound of approaching footsteps. She shoved Robert's bathrobe into her backpack to study later and ran out into the hallway, seconds before a white-haired chambermaid appeared.

"May I help you?" the maid asked in a distracted voice. Elizabeth saw tearstains on her face and knew she was grieving for the murdered cook. "It's Miss Jessica Wakefield, isn't it?"

"That's right," Elizabeth said, trying to control her excited breathing. She smiled tentatively, showing the dimple in her left cheek. "I'm afraid I'm lost in this big house," she said solemnly. "Can you direct me to, uh, the library?"

The library was the first thing that popped into Elizabeth's head, and she wanted to kick herself as soon as she said it. Nobody who knew Jessica would believe she was searching for a library.

Elizabeth let out a sigh of relief as the maid gave her directions. *Of course, nobody here knows Jessica well enough to be suspicious of a statement like that.*

Like every room at Pembroke Manor, the Pembroke library was richly decorated in a style Elizabeth thought of as very

English. This room had a masculine look, with a big mahogany desk in one corner and accents of burgundy leather everywhere. Grouped on the desk and arranged on one wall was a collection of formal family portraits in gilt-edged wood frames.

But the books were what held Elizabeth's attention. She pulled out a copy of *Wuthering Heights*—a first edition, she was sure—and lovingly fingered its well-dusted leather spine. Then she pushed it back onto the shelf, forcing herself to remember her mission. She began looking for clues.

When she saw Robert Louis Stevenson's *The Strange Case of Dr. Jekyll and Mr. Hyde*, Elizabeth forgot her resolve once more. She had started to read the book last week at HIS and hadn't had a chance to get back to it since. Well, Pembroke had told her to make herself at home. Perhaps he wouldn't mind if she borrowed it for the evening to read in bed. She reached up and began to pull the book from the shelf.

Elizabeth heard a loud click. She whirled around guiltily, and her eyes widened with astonishment. A leather-covered panel in the wall had sprung open. Pulling out the volume had triggered a secret door!

"Even the walls here aren't what they seem," she whispered breathlessly.

Then Elizabeth pushed open the secret door and walked slowly into the small, dark room.

Elizabeth groped for a light switch and stared around her. The secret room was a small, book-lined study.

Animal skins and heads adorned the walls, as in the dining room. But the dining-room animals were from African safaris. The animals in this room were wolves leering down at her with their teeth bared.

"The wolves' den!" she whispered, spooked.

The room was stuffy, but Elizabeth shivered.

She caught sight of some of the titles of the leather-bound books, and her mouth dropped open. It seemed that every book in the room had something to do with were-wolves. She suppressed a shudder. "Lord Pembroke must be some kind of werewolf fanatic," she whispered, more because of the eeriness of the room than out of a fear of being discovered. "How creepy!"

Then she remembered that Luke was also a serious student of werewolf lore. But, she told herself loyally, there was nothing creepy about Luke's fascination with the subject—not like Lord Pembroke's obsession. Collecting werewolf books and wolf heads and hiding them in a secret room was downright weird.

Still, Elizabeth had to admit that Luke would love this place. She couldn't wait to tell him about it.

For a moment Elizabeth considered calling him. She eyed the telephone that sat on a small, cluttered desk in the center of the room. Then she shook her head. Her time for searching for clues was too limited to spend it talking on the phone; she would tell Luke later. But she did notice that the phone number was not the one she had used to call Pembroke that morning. The werewolf room was so secret, it even had its own telephone number. She wondered if that was to keep people from picking up other extensions in the house and hearing Pembroke's private conversations.

Elizabeth turned to the crowded bookshelves and scanned the titles. Unlike the well-kept volumes in Lord Pembroke's main library, most of the books in the werewolf room were blanketed with a layer of dust. Obviously, not even the servants knew about this room.

Elizabeth selected a beautifully bound volume, a sixteenth-century French work called *Discours de la Lycanthropie.* "Discourses on Lycanthropy," she translated aloud. Before coming to England, she had never heard of lycanthropy. Now she knew the term was used both for the study of werewolves and for the delusion that a person has turned into a wolf. The book fell open in Elizabeth's hands. She blew the fine powder from the title page and read an inscription written in graceful, elongated script: "To Robert. With all my love, Annabelle."

The inscription was dated twenty years earlier, so Elizabeth knew the words had been written to the elder Lord Pembroke rather than his son. "But who is Annabelle?" she asked aloud. The inscription sounded as if it had been written by a lover—but certainly Lord and Lady Pembroke had been married at the time; Robert was twenty years old.

But Lady Pembroke's first name was not Annabelle.

Elizabeth's imagination began to race. Had Lord Pembroke and Annabelle had a tragic love affair twenty years earlier? Was that the scandal Eliana had mentioned? And where was Annabelle now?

For a moment Elizabeth felt a twinge of sympathy for Lord Pembroke, but she pushed it aside, chastising herself for being too sentimental. She was here to solve a mystery and capture a killer, not to moon over a twenty-year-old romance.

Elizabeth stared thoughtfully at the inscription. "Could Annabelle be the key to the mystery?" she asked herself.

Elizabeth didn't know, but she was determined to find the answers.

Elizabeth leaned over Lord Pembroke's ornately carved mahogany desk early on Wednesday morning. Her search of the library and werewolf room had been interrupted the day before when a servant came to dust the library. Elizabeth had barely made it out of the hidden room in time.

Elizabeth hadn't seen Lord Pembroke since her arrival the day before; she hoped he was still in bed that morning. Certainly Maria's murder had made Pembroke forget all about the interview he was supposed to have with "Jessica" today. But that was fine with Elizabeth. She thought she had a better chance of finding something useful if she could manage some uninterrupted time for sleuthing around Pembroke Manor.

So far Elizabeth's trip had been successful. The green robe was circumstantial evidence, but it did implicate Robert for Joy's murder. And the werewolf room was interesting, though Elizabeth wasn't sure how Lord Pembroke's obsession with werewolves tied in to the murders. What did it mean? Had Lord Pembroke known all along that his son was a werewolf? Was his study of lycanthropy an effort to understand more about Robert's condition? No, she decided. The date on Annabelle's gift book proved that Pembroke had been interested in werewolves at least since the time of Robert's birth. So what did it all mean?

Elizabeth sighed. Despite her discoveries, she still hadn't found solid proof that the younger Robert Pembroke was a werewolf and a murderer. But time was running out; her train would leave for London in a few hours.

"Annabelle," she said aloud, thinking of the inscription on the werewolf book. "I don't know why, but I know she's important to all of this."

Elizabeth slowly opened the top drawer of Pembroke's desk and immediately saw what she was looking for—an address book.

"Annabelle," she said again, thumbing through the pages as quickly as she could. "Why couldn't Annabelle have signed her last name on her inscription, too?"

She laid the address book back in the drawer and sighed heavily. Of the entries that listed first names, not a single one mentioned an Annabelle. Then she turned and scrutinized the shelves until she saw what looked like a college yearbook. From the date on the spine, she guessed it was Pembroke's yearbook.

"Oxford," she said. "Naturally."

She flipped through the pages until she found his photograph.

"Lettered in crew and polo," she read. "Debating Society, Dramatics Society, Hunt Club."

Not much help there. Elizabeth leafed through the back section of the book, where several pages had been left blank for signatures. She scanned the pages for the elegant, elongated handwriting she had memorized from the inscription in the werewolf book. There was no Annabelle.

"I guess I'll try the wolves' den one last time," she said under her breath, reaching for the copy of *Jekyll and Hyde* that she now knew would trigger the secret door.

As her fingers grazed the volume, Elizabeth froze. She could hear Lord Pembroke's voice, just outside the library doors.

Elizabeth dove under the mahogany desk as Pembroke strolled into the room followed by Andrew Thatcher. Then she clapped her hand over her mouth in consternation—the secret door had clicked open and was standing slightly ajar. If Pembroke or Thatcher noticed it, they would surely discover her.

"Yesterday's murder was the last straw," Thatcher said after he had closed the double doors behind them. Elizabeth noticed that the police chief looked thinner and more haggard than just a couple days earlier. Joy's death was apparently taking its toll on him. "I know we agreed that the killer would be apprehended more quickly if we kept it out of the newspapers. And that due to your expertise you would, in a sense, carry on your own investigation." He ran his hand through his dark hair, making it stand on end. "But I can't risk any more lives, Robert. We have to bring this monster in. My detectives at Scotland Yard are breathing down my neck. They suspect that you know more than you're telling—and I think so, too."

Pembroke began pacing. Elizabeth held her breath as he approached the secret door; she let it out, relieved, as he passed by the door without stopping.

"Just a little more time, Andrew," Pembroke pleaded. "We've known each other since boyhood—trust me for a few more days. You know that we're onto something big here, but we can't afford to play our hand too early."

"We can't afford to wait!" Thatcher yelled. "Four people have died! How many more will it take? I know you have evidence of who it is—"

"But, Andrew," Pembroke argued.

"Don't try to deny it," Thatcher said. "I've gone along with you until now, but no longer. I don't care how long we've been friends. Robert, I have to know what you know. Tell me who the evidence points to, and hand over any clues you have—regardless of who they implicate."

Pembroke shook his head nervously. "I don't think that's a good idea. The evidence I've found is misleading. It points to an innocent man!"

What evidence can he have? Elizabeth wondered, thinking of the large portrait of Robert on the wall. *Does Lord Pembroke suspect Robert, too?* Then she cringed as he passed near the partially open door to the werewolf room.

"That's what police investigations are for," Thatcher said. "You just hand over the evidence and let us decide if it warrants an arrest. Don't worry. We'll have to be bloody sure of the evidence before we accuse a man of being a werewolf!"

Elizabeth's eyes widened. Pembroke and Thatcher had known all along about the werewolf!

"But if I have all the evidence," Thatcher continued, "I can put out a warrant for the suspect's arrest. Then we can question him and arrive at the truth of the matter."

Pembroke sat down heavily in the desk chair, and Thatcher took over the pacing. Beneath the desk, Elizabeth scooted as far away from his knees as she could get, plastering her body against the opposite side.

For a moment Pembroke sat with his elbows on the mahogany surface, cradling his forehead in his hands.

"All right," he said reluctantly, his voice muffled. "I'll turn over the evidence. But not right now. Let me talk to him first." He hesitated. "Perhaps I can coax him to quietly turn himself in for questioning—although, as I told you, I'm certain he's innocent."

He pushed the chair out from the desk and turned to Thatcher. The police chief stopped pacing and stood with his arms folded—directly in front of the door to the werewolf room.

Elizabeth stiffened, willing the police chief not to turn around and see that the leather-covered panel was slightly open.

"I'll allow you until ten o'clock tonight to give me the evidence," Thatcher said. "But that's it! If you can convince your friend to turn himself in, then perhaps the law will go easier on him. But if you even think about changing your mind, Robert, remember that I can subpoena you to turn over any evidence you've found."

Pembroke nodded wordlessly.

"Our friendship is important to me,

Robert," Thatcher said. "But you know I could lose my job if anyone finds out I've been allowing you to withhold evidence."

"I understand, Andrew. And I appreciate your cooperation. You're a good friend."

Thatcher strode across the room to the double doors of the library and then turned to face Pembroke again. "Do me a favor, Robert," he said. "Tell Reeves to ease up on the princess hype. It's making us look like we're not doing our job!"

After the police chief had left, Lord Pembroke stood in front of Robert's portrait. "The evidence must be wrong," he said in a determined voice. "My son is not a killer—or a werewolf! I refuse to believe it. I'll clear your name, Robert," he vowed, eyes fierce with determination. "I promise I will."

Lord Pembroke stared up at his son's portrait, slowly shaking his head. Robert was innocent. Of that, he had no doubt.

Perhaps he was misinterpreting the evidence he'd found—the cigarette case from the Essex Street murder site and the green threads from Robert's silk bathrobe. Or perhaps someone else had planted the evidence in order to frame his son. But who would do such a thing? And why?

The only thing he knew for sure was that he couldn't let the police arrest his son. Robert was no murderer. And Pembroke had promised himself years earlier that he would never let another scandal rock the Pembroke family name.

"I must warn Robert before I talk to Thatcher," he decided aloud. "He must disappear for a bit—allow me time to find the real werewolf."

He reached across the desk for the telephone, but then changed his mind. For this call, he needed the complete privacy of his hidden room, with its separate phone line. It would never do for a bumbling servant to happen upon him at an inopportune point in the conversation. *Too many people are investigating this case already*, he told himself, thinking about Jessica Wakefield's nosy sister scribbling in that notebook of hers. He would make the call from his secret study.

Pembroke reached for *The Strange Case of Dr. Jekyll and Mr. Hyde* to trigger the hidden door. Then he froze. The leather-covered panel was already open.

"That's odd," he said aloud, fighting

down a feeling of panic. "I'm certain I didn't leave that door ajar." But nobody else even knew of the existence of the wolf den—not even his wife. "Annabelle is the only other soul who ever knew about this room, and that was years ago."

He stood in the doorway and gazed around his private study. Nothing seemed to have been disturbed. In fact, he felt the same rush of emotion that always engulfed him upon entering the secret room—an odd mixture of security, mystery, and passion. He and Annabelle had spent so many happy hours there, examining old documents and discovering new theories.

But the concerns of the present were too disturbing to allow more than a moment of nostalgia. Somebody else had discovered his room. Perhaps one of the servants had pulled out *Jekyll and Hyde* while dusting, he told himself. He would have to investigate—after he called Robert.

He closed the hidden door carefully behind him as he walked into the little room.

Lord Pembroke had another mystery on his hands.

*   *   *

As soon as Lord Pembroke disappeared into the secret study, Elizabeth jumped out from under the mahogany desk and raced from the library. She leaped up the stairs, two at a time, to reach the telephone in the hallway outside her room. The information she had just overheard couldn't wait; she had to call Luke right away and fill him in on everything she had learned. It was lucky that the telephone Lord Pembroke was using in the werewolf den was on a separate line.

Elizabeth tapped her foot impatiently as the phone rang repeatedly on Luke's desk at the *Journal*.

"Rats!" she said aloud. "Where could he be?"

She dialed the twins' boss at the newspaper, Tony's number instead.

"I'm not completely certain where Luke is this morning, Liz," Tony replied to her urgent question. "Out and about on an arts and entertainment scoop, no doubt. I've actually been able to get a lot of work done, with you and Luke out on your various stories and Jessica spending the day with that young nobleman of hers—"

Elizabeth broke out in a cold sweat. *"Jessica is where?"*

"I assumed you knew," Tony said. "She took a holiday today to spend some time with the young Lord Pembroke. She didn't mention where they would be going."

Elizabeth's hands were trembling as she replaced the telephone receiver. Jessica was alone all day with a killer—and probably a werewolf!

Elizabeth knew she had to return to London immediately. She had to find Jessica—before it was too late.

I guess it's obvious that Jessica and I both survived London, but I still get chills when I think about that summer.

Jessica's put me on the defensive by bringing up all of the twin switches I've pulled. She's probably had to wrack her brain to come up with these couple of occasions when I've been the one sneaking around. She's done it dozens of times.

There was this one time in particular, during our freshman year at Sweet Valley University, when she pulled a switch that made me so mad, I almost killed her. . . .

PART FOUR

You don't have to be a genius science nerd to figure out which incident Elizabeth is talking about. Maybe I did go a little too far, but I still don't see how what I did was so wrong.

We don't dwell on it now, but the fact is, Elizabeth had a very hard time adjusting to college life. She just couldn't get a grip on the idea that we weren't living in our cozy house on Calico Drive anymore. I mean, the girl practically refused to have a good time. And if she hadn't been so stubborn, I wouldn't have been forced to go to the Homecoming football game with Peter Wilbourne the Third in the first place—

Hold on. Rewind. Let me tell you how it happened from the beginning. From the mo-

ment I knew what going to college even meant (aside from the hideous academic part of it), I wanted to be a Theta. The Thetas are the best sorority on campus, and my mother was a Theta, and so on. Elizabeth and I were shoo-ins, except for the fact that she had to go making major trouble at the first big Sigma party of the year. The Sigma house is the most elite fraternity at SVU, and if they don't like you, your social rep is pretty much in the toilet.

As you may have guessed, Elizabeth likes to take on every good cause she runs across. And I admire that about her. I really do. But sometimes it's very inconvenient. The night of the Sigma party my date was a gorgeous African-American guy, Danny Wyatt. Well, Danny and I were dancing, and this really obnoxious and terrible guy, Peter Wilbourne (who also happened to be president of the Sigmas) started harassing Danny and me.

It seems Danny and Peter had a long-standing hatred for one another, and the fact that Peter is a racist pig made the situation worse. So Liz heard Peter going off on Danny (I won't repeat the vile things he said), and she stood up in front of the whole party and really gave Peter an earful. He was furious.

Peter made it his personal duty to get Liz

back for making him look like a fool, which is
what resulted in me, or should I say, Elizabeth,
being at the game with Satan—I mean, Peter.

Alarm bells should have rung in my head as
soon as my roommate, Isabella Ricci, told me
that the vice president of the Thetas, Alison
Quinn, had been by to see me. Stupid me, I re-
mained calm. Isabella informed me that in order
to atone for her un-Theta-like behavior at the
Sigma party, Elizabeth had to publicly apolo-
gize to Big Man On Campus, Peter Wilbourne.
Or else. Like I said, I needed to be a Theta the
way I need air. . . .

"Alison Quinn was looking for you,"
Isabella Ricci said to Jessica.

"Alison Quinn," Jessica said, looking
puzzled. "What did she want? I already
know I'm being pledged to the Thetas."

"She wanted to talk to you about
Elizabeth. She wants you to tell Elizabeth
what she has to do to prove her loyalty to
the Thetas."

"I don't know what she has to do,"
Jessica said, stifling a yawn.

Isabella picked up a pale violet envelope
with the silver sorority insignia on it. "You
do now," she said, handing it to her.

77

Isabella watched Jessica reading the note, waiting for her reaction. She'd expected Jessica to be as outraged and horrified as she was, but she'd been wrong. The sea-green eyes looked a little dismayed; that was all.

Jessica tossed the violet notepaper aside as though it were no more than a shopping list. "I'll talk to Liz this afternoon. She's going to take some convincing—I mean, she isn't exactly Peter Wilbourne's biggest fan—but I'm sure she'll come around." She got up and stretched.

"Is that it?" asked Isabella.

"Is what it?"

"Is that all you have to say about it? After the way Peter Wilbourne treated you and Danny, and the way the Sigmas harassed you and Elizabeth, is that all you can say? 'She'll come around'?"

Jessica looked baffled. "What do you want me to say? That I won't join the Thetas because they want my sister to go out with Peter the Creep?"

"No," Isabella said, shaking her head. "I don't want you to drop the sorority, Jess. I just thought you'd be a little angry—you know, that you might stand up to Alison."

"Stand up to Alison—are you nuts, Isabella? The Thetas would drop me in a second if I did that."

"Not necessarily," Isabella argued. "You might convince them to give Elizabeth some other kind of test."

"*Might*," Jessica said, "And they *might* not." She started toward the bathroom. "Well, it's not a chance I'm willing to take. Joining the Thetas is too important to me."

Jessica was singing along to the love song playing on her Walkman as she entered Dickenson Hall, the dorm where her sister lived. Her argument with Isabella was already forgotten and her good mood restored.

By now Jessica had not only forgotten her argument with her roommate, she'd also convinced herself that the Thetas' request was really no big deal. So Elizabeth had to go out with Peter Wilbourne, so what? There wasn't a woman in the world who didn't go out with a complete creep now and then. It was the hazard of dating. You could never be sure that the guy who seemed okay when he asked you to the movies wouldn't turn out to be some loser who snored in the middle of the film or who spent the night talking about megabytes and binary-object files.

Jessica had had dozens of dates with guys just as bad as Peter Wilbourne III. She'd thought at the time the dates would never end, that she'd never survive, but when she looked back on them, they actually made her laugh. Elizabeth would go out with Peter for a few gruesome hours, and later she would laugh about it. "Remember the time I went out with that noxious waste, Peter Wilbourne?" she'd say. "Remember when I had to publicly apologize for telling the world what a septic tank he was? Wasn't that the funniest thing?"

Jessica didn't bother to knock.

Elizabeth was sitting at her desk, concentrating on something she was writing. She looked up as Jessica floated in, pulling off her headset and letting a fizzle of music into the room.

"I knew I'd find my beautiful twin here, working away like a slave on this beautiful autumn day," Jessica said.

Elizabeth looked from Jessica to the window and back again. "It's raining, Jess," she said. "It may be beautiful out if you're a walrus, but for most of us humans a heavy downpour is less than ideal."

"Oh, come on, Liz." Jessica dropped her wet jacket on Elizabeth's bed and sat on the edge of her desk. "Didn't some poet say something about beauty depending on who's seeing it?" she asked.

Elizabeth smiled. "Something like that."

"Well?" Jessica raised her arms expansively. "When I look outside, I see a beautiful day!"

"I'm glad to hear that, Jess, but I wish you'd sit somewhere else." Elizabeth gave her a little shove. "You're wrinkling my notes."

"Oh, pardon me! I wouldn't want to be responsible for wrinkling your notes." Jessica slid to the floor, dragging several pages covered with Elizabeth's handwriting with her. She reached down to retrieve them. "Don't you ever get tired of doing work all the time?" she asked, not even bothering to glance at them as she put them back on the desk.

Elizabeth gave her an exasperated look. "It's an assignment for the station."

"So, do you have a date for the Homecoming game?" Jessica asked, deciding to cut to the chase.

Elizabeth started writing again. "I'm not going to the game. I want to work on this as much as I can."

"I think you may be wrong about that," Jessica said, using her little-sister voice.

Elizabeth didn't look up. "Forget it, Jess. I don't care if you got yourself two dates for the game and you need me to take one of them—I'm not doing it. I'm staying here and working."

"But Liz . . ." Jessica crouched beside her sister's chair. "It's not that, it's much more important than that. My whole social life at SVU is on the line here."

Elizabeth stopped mid-word and looked at her. Jessica hated it when her sister stared at her like that, as if she could read her thoughts and didn't like what she saw. "This doesn't have something to do with the Thetas, does it?"

How did Elizabeth know things like that? Jessica forced herself to smile. "They just want you to do one little thing to prove your loyalty."

"What little thing?" Elizabeth asked, not returning her smile.

"They just want you to go to the game with Peter Wilbourne," Jessica said in a rush. She was convinced that if she got it out fast enough, Elizabeth wouldn't object as much. "And apologize for reaming him out in public that time."

Elizabeth was looking at her as though she were sprouting fur and fangs.

"They what?"

"They want you—"

"Jessica Wakefield, have you lost your mind completely?" Elizabeth stood up so quickly that Jessica fell over. "You can't seriously think that I'd go out with Peter Wilbourne!"

"Think of it this way, Liz," Jessica said reasonably, getting to her feet. "You haven't had one date since you've been here. Even though you don't like Peter Wilbourne, it can't hurt your reputation to be seen with the president of the Sigmas."

Elizabeth stared at her. "You are crazy," she said slowly. "You are out of your tiny mind."

"Oh, come on, Liz. It's only one date. A football game doesn't last that long, *and* it's all outdoors. All you have to do is sit there and watch the game and drink a soda and that's it. You don't even have to talk to him, except to apologize—which won't take a second. What could be simpler?"

Elizabeth shook her head. "Unbelievable. After the way that moron treated you and Danny . . . I just can't believe, I cannot believe you'd even suggest this."

"Liz, the Thetas will change their minds about pledging me if they change their minds about pledging you, and they'll definitely change their minds about you if you don't do this one little thing."

"I won't do it, Jessica."

Jessica started to wheedle. "Liz, be reasonable. This isn't the end of the world, you know. It's one lousy little date. You've been on bad dates before. You'll laugh about this later, Liz. I guarantee it. Years from now, all I'll have to say is 'Peter Wilbourne' and you'll go into hysterics."

But Elizabeth was way beyond wheedling.

"The only reason I've gone this far with the Thetas is because of you," she said calmly. "But this is where I stop. It's bad enough being on the same planet with a scum like Peter Wilbourne; there is *no way* I'm going to date him. And there is ab-

84

solutely no way in the universe that I would *apologize* to him."

Steven came racing up the bleacher stairs with a cardboard tray filled with hot dogs, sodas, and popcorn. "This is the life!" he exclaimed as he sat down beside Billie. "A beautiful autumn day, a beautiful Homecoming game, and a beautiful woman to share them both with." He leaned over and kissed her. For today, at least, Steven had decided to put his concern for his sisters out of his mind and to have a good time.

"Never mind all that soppy stuff," Billie teased, kissing him back. "Unhand my frank."

Steven laughed, suddenly realizing that this was the most relaxed he'd felt in weeks. *Since the beginning of the term*, he told himself. *Since Elizabeth and Jessica arrived.*

Billie poked him with her elbow. "Stop it," she ordered.

"Stop what?" he asked innocently.

"Stop thinking about your sisters. You promised you wouldn't think about them all afternoon. You swore the only thing in your head would be football and me."

Steven grinned. "How did you know I was thinking about them?"

She gave him a wry smile. "Because you get the exact same look on your face my father used to get when I first started going out with boys."

"Well, Ms. Detective," Steven said. "It just might interest you to know that I wasn't really thinking about them. I was thinking how good it felt not to worry about them for a couple of hours."

"Well, stop thinking about it and just enjoy it. This is going to be a great game." She kissed his cheek.

"It's a great game already," Steven said, putting his arm around her. "And it hasn't even started yet."

He bit into his hot dog and gazed happily across the stands. It looked as though the entire school had turned out for it. He saw his sociology professor, three of his good friends from the prelaw program, Billie's friend Sandi and her boyfriend, and he saw Elizabeth and Peter Wilbourne.

The hot dog turned to sand in Steven's mouth. He gave Billie a shake. "Billie, look over there! Where those Thetas are sitting. Tell me what you see."

Billie followed the direction his hand was pointing. "I see Elizabeth and Peter Wilbourne."

Steven turned to her, disbelief on his face. "And that seems all right to you?"

Billie shrugged. "It seems a little strange. I thought Elizabeth didn't like Peter, but I guess she changed her mind."

"Billie," Steven said, fighting to remain calm. "Nobody with half a brain likes Peter. The guy's a power-happy bigot with an ego as big as Alaska."

She eyed him warily. "Oh, don't get started on him now, Steven."

"Well, it doesn't make me happy." He threw his hot dog back in the tray. "What is it with my sisters? Jessica's always been a little flaky, especially when it comes to boys, but Elizabeth was always rational. Elizabeth—"

"Steven!" Billie looked as if she were about to dump her soda over his head. "Stop it! When are you going to accept the fact that your sisters are adults now, and that they can go out whomever they want? They have to take responsibility for their own lives."

*   *   *

"I don't mind admitting when I've been wrong," the girl who looked, acted, and sounded exactly like Elizabeth Wakefield was saying in a loud, clear voice. "And I was wrong about you, Peter. I was very wrong, and I'm sorry." She took Peter Wilbourne's hand. "I'm really and truly sorry."

Isabella smiled to herself. She had to hand it to Jessica—she was so convincing as her twin that even Isabella could believe she was Elizabeth.

"I accept your apology," Peter said solemnly. "And I forgive you." He pulled her to him. "Let's kiss and make up. You know it's what you've wanted all along."

The group of Thetas and Sigmas whistled and cheered.

After that kiss it wasn't easy for Jessica to convince Peter Wilbourne that she didn't want to spend the rest of the afternoon with him. Thank God, he already had a date for the Homecoming dance or he would have expected her to go to that with him, too. Jessica shuddered as she raced away after the game, like Cinderella running out of the ball. She'd had about as much of Peter Wilbourne III as she could take for one lifetime. He had to be the most egotistical bore she'd ever met.

But all's well that ends well, Jessica told herself as she strode toward her dorm. *It was just like the dentist. You hate going, but when it's all over, you feel better.*

Alison had congratulated her as she was leaving on being pledged to the Thetas. "I can admit when I'm wrong, too," Alison had said. "I think both you and Jessica will make terrific Thetas, and so does everyone else."

"We're sorry to barge in like this," Billie said as she sat down on Elizabeth's bed. "But you know what these big dances are like. Steven was afraid we wouldn't even have a chance to say hello to you if we didn't stop by on our way."

Steven shoved some of her roommate's things to one side and positioned himself gingerly on the edge of her desk.

"Don't apologize," Elizabeth answered sincerely. "It's really good to see you."

Billie chatted happily about the evening ahead, asking Elizabeth what she thought about her hair and her dress and complaining that her shoes were too tight. But

Steven was looking at Elizabeth in a way that he usually reserved for Jessica: perplexed, frustrated, disappointed.

"Why aren't you dressed?" he asked when Billie's voice finally trailed off into silence. "Won't Peter Wilbourne be picking you up soon?"

Elizabeth's smile disappeared. "What?"

Steven was drumming his fingers on the desktop the way Mr. Wakefield did when he was upset about something. "You heard me," he said shortly. "You went to the game with Peter the Geek. Considering the way you were kissing him right there in broad daylight, I assumed you'd be going to the dance with him, too."

Elizabeth could feel something going very wrong with her blood. It was turning to ice. "What?" she whispered.

Billie stood up. "Steven, you promised . . ."

Steven stood up, too, refusing even to glance at Billie. "Come on, Liz. We saw you. Practically the whole school saw you." He shook his head. "After the way he treated you and Jess— I just can't *believe* you'd go out with a creep like that."

Billie's voice was sharp. "Steven—"

Elizabeth cut her off. "What are you

talking about? I wouldn't go out with Peter Wilbourne if he was the last man on earth. I've been in this room the entire day."

Steven stared at her. Elizabeth stared back. The truth hit them both at exactly the same moment.

"Jessica!"

Billie let out her breath. "What a relief," she said, slipping her arm into Steven's. "Your brother's been driving me crazy because he thought you were going out with Peter."

Elizabeth wasn't relieved. She was furious. Of all the low-down, sneaky things her twin had done to her in the last eighteen years, this had to be the worst. Knowing how strongly Elizabeth felt about Peter, Jessica had gone ahead and impersonated her just so she could get into some obnoxious, stuck-up sorority.

"Elizabeth?" Steven said. Both he and Billie were looking at her with concern. "Are you okay? You look like you're about to explode."

Elizabeth's eyes were flashing and her jaw was set. "I am about to explode," she said. "I can't believe she did that to me. After I told her I wouldn't go out with him,

91

not under any circumstances, no matter what the stupid Thetas wanted—" She broke off, too furious to go on.

Steven came over and put a hand on her shoulder. "I'll talk to her, Liz. Jessica's been getting pretty carried away with herself lately. I want to try to reason with her if I can."

Suddenly Billie was standing beside him. "Why can't you let them work out their own problems?" she demanded. She picked up her bag from Elizabeth's desk. "Why do you have to interfere all the time?"

"Billie's right," Elizabeth said quickly. She didn't want Steven talking to Jessica. She wanted to wring Jessica's neck herself. "I'll handle Jess. Believe me, I know exactly what I want to say."

Thank goodness, Liz eventually forgave me. And by the time she got through with Peter Wilbourne, he knew not to mess with the mighty Elizabeth Wakefield. But I knew Elizabeth would forgive me. She had to. The truth of the matter is, Liz and I are as close as any two people can be. I need her. She needs me. Alone, neither of us is half as strong as we are together. I think there's an algebra equation in there some-where, but I'll let Elizabeth try to figure it out. I've got to get to the beach, where a certain life-guard is pining away, waiting for me. . . .

If you enjoyed reading about Elizabeth's private thoughts, don't miss *Elizabeth's Secret Diary*. Elizabeth goes through a lot of changes during her junior year in high school—she even has to contend with Todd moving away to Vermont. Elizabeth vows to be true to Todd, but letters and phone calls aren't as satisfying as she'd hoped. Will Elizabeth start dating handsome Nicholas Morrow? Or will she fill the void of Todd's absence with the most forbidden fruit of all—her boyfriend's best friend, Ken Matthews? Read this special sneak preview of *Elizabeth's Secret Diary* and learn things about

Elizabeth Wakefield that will blow your mind. . . .

Saturday, midnight

Ken called me this afternoon and we went to a movie tonight. It almost seemed like a Saturday-night date, but of course he's just looking after me as Todd asked him to. Still, when he dropped me off at my house afterward, I was startled by the way I felt as I looked into his eyes to say good-bye. . . .

"This was a lot of fun," I told Ken as we stood on the front step of my house. "Really. I don't know when I've had such a good time."

It was true. We'd had a riot at the movie, a horror film that kept us both on the edge of our seats the whole time. Then we'd gone to Guido's for a pizza, where we'd chattered for hours about every topic under the sun.

"My pleasure," Ken said with a grin. "I love going to scary movies with a girl who doesn't shriek and dig holes in my arm with her fingernails."

I laughed. "I *did* shriek at one part."

"Yeah, but I was screaming, too, so I didn't notice."

"Well . . ." I looked up at Ken. His blond hair glimmered in the moonlight; there was a warm glow in his eyes. My breath caught in my throat, and I felt my heart thump with extra force. For an instant, gazing into Ken's eyes, I knew how Suzanne felt when she was with him. I knew why she'd clung to Ken so stubbornly even though they weren't right for each other. *She probably looked up at him in the moonlight, just like this*, I thought, *and he was so handsome and strong, she just wanted him to wrap her in his arms and never let go. . . .*

"Well, good night," I squeaked, clutching the doorknob.

"'Night, Liz."

Ken put a hand on my arm. What were we supposed to do now? Shake hands? Peck each other on the cheek? I turned back to face him and he gave me a quick hug. I hugged him back, laughing to hide my awkwardness. "See you in school, Ken."

With a good-bye wave, he sauntered down the walk to his car, which was parked by the curb. I followed him with my eyes, drinking in the graceful lines of his broad, muscular back, his long, lean legs. A shiver chased up my spine. *That's Ken Matthews you're thinking about,* I chastised myself as I slipped into the front hall. *Your buddy. Todd's best friend. So cut it out!*

I must be tired, I decided as I tiptoed up the stairs. *I must be feeling especially weak and vulnerable.* Because my heart was still doing backflips; there were goose bumps on my arms from where Ken had touched me.

> *Pretty weird, huh, Diary? If I didn't know better, I'd think I was falling for Ken. But it's just because we've been spending so much time together—talking about Todd, mostly! I feel especially close to him these days.*

Sunday, 6:45 P.M.

Dear Diary,

Right before dinner I picked up the phone to call Ken to see if he'd heard from Todd, then hung up without dialing. Was that really the reason I was calling him?

Friday, 12:30 A.M.

The Friday-the-thirteenth dance was fun. Ken and I danced just about every song together. Usually I miss Todd at events like this, but tonight I have to confess I didn't think of him once. . . .

"Let's take a break and sit one out," I suggested to Ken as the DJ put on a slow song. "I'm pretty breathless, aren't you?"

The mood in the gym had changed along with the music. All around us couples drew closer, wrapping their arms around each other. Romance seemed to fill the air like a perfume.

Ken grasped my arm, preventing me from stepping away. "One more," he said. "Slow dances aren't too strenuous!"

Laughing, I stepped close again. Ken put his arms around my shoulders and I circled mine around his waist. Gingerly I rested my head against his chest. *Have we ever slow danced before?* I found myself wondering. I didn't think so. I didn't think I'd ever been this physically close to Ken Matthews. . . .

He was right—slow dancing wasn't that strenuous. But for some reason I still felt breathless. Why was my pulse racing? Why was my face so hot?

"You know, Ken," I murmured, not meeting his eyes, "you should ask some other girls to dance. I know you're just looking out for me, but I'll be OK."

Ken's arms tightened around me. "What if I don't *want* to ask other girls to dance? What if I only want to dance with you?"

We were silent, our bodies swaying together to the slow, sensuous music. I couldn't answer Ken's question; I wouldn't. What if . . . ?

I know what's happening to me, Diary. I wasn't born yesterday—I've had feelings like this before. But I can't give in to them. Ken is Todd's best friend! I have to nip this in the bud. But it's hard. When Ken's arms were around me, my body pressed against his . . . I could feel his heart pounding—we were both generating an awful lot of heat. Thank God, no one noticed.

He offered to drive me home, but I turned him down and I hope he knows why. I hope he's making a resolution, too—we simply can't follow up on this attraction. It'll pass if we ignore it.

Aaron Dallas brought this new guy with him tonight. His name is Jeffrey French—he just moved here from Oregon and he's starting at SVH on Monday. He and Aaron knew each other from soccer camp, or that's the story going around, anyway. I think Enid may have fallen in love with Jeffrey at first sight—one glance at him and she was incoherent for the rest of the night! He is pretty cute—tall, blond, athletic—but frankly, I had a hard time focusing on him. My gaze kept straying to another tall, blond, athletic guy, initials K.M. . . . DON'T DO THIS, LIZ!!!

Saturday night, late

Dear Diary,

I almost didn't want to write this down. I hope no one ever finds out about it. I can't believe I let myself get so carried away at Lila's party tonight. . . .

Ken and I were in the kitchen; he was helping me load up another platter with foot-long submarine sandwiches. I unwrapped the last sandwich; the platter was

ready to go. "There," I announced some-
what unnecessarily.

Ken and I looked at each other.
Something in Ken's eyes told me I should
take a step backward, away from him.

"Liz," he said, his voice deep.

He clasped my hand and my resolve
melted. Instead of backing away I let him
pull me outside to the patio.

The backyard was dark, and we slipped
eagerly into the shadows. Without another
word Ken folded his arms around me, lift-
ing me slightly so his mouth could find
mine. I kissed him hungrily, my fingers
tangling in his hair. Meanwhile, his hands
were on my neck, my shoulders, my back.
We couldn't seem to stop touching each
other—maybe because for weeks we'd
been dying to do this, but holding back.

After a long, recklessly delicious moment, I pulled away, breathless. "Ken, we
really shouldn't—"

"Ssh." He placed a finger gently against my
lips. "Don't say it. Let's not think about . . ."

It was too late. It was already out there.
Guilt crept into my heart, momentarily
chilling my passion. Todd trusted Ken and
me—how could we do this to him?

Ken reached for me again. If his hand so much as brushed my skin, I knew I'd throw myself back into his arms. Whirling, I ran away, back into the house.

Where will this end, Diary? Because it's finally started. Ken and I have let our feelings for each other show. There's no going back now. . . .

                      Sunday, 11:00 P.M.

Dear Diary,
   Todd called this morning. I couldn't believe the timing—it's almost as if he knew. But of course he doesn't; he was perfectly cheerful and casual. "So is Ken looking after you like I asked him to?" he actually said. I just about died. When I answered, I was sure he'd hear the guilt in my voice, but he didn't seem to suspect anything. Why should he? I'm his girlfriend, and Ken's his best buddy. If he can't trust us, who can he trust?
   "It won't happen again"—that was what I was telling myself when I hung up the phone with Todd. I decided there was one surefire way to get rid of the guilt: stay away from Ken. It was just

one kiss, after all—Todd probably kissed that Diane girl after the dance, so that makes us even. It wasn't too late to draw a line with Ken—I knew he'd agree with me that it was the best thing to do. We'd just pretend it never happened.

Who was I kidding?? I might as well have told the ocean to stop crashing on the shore. I had to see Ken, and he felt the same way. We met at the beach tonight—I told my family I was going over to Olivia's to study for the French test. Diary, I've never felt so bad—and so good—at the same time. . . .

"I think we should talk about this," I said to Ken as we fell together onto the beach blanket he'd just spread out in the shelter of a sand dune.

Ken kissed my face, my throat. "Go ahead," he whispered, his lips near my ear. "I'm listening."

The night wind sighed through the dune grass; just a few yards away the surf crashed rhythmically on the sand. "Oh, Ken, I . . ." I held him close, burying my face against his neck. "This is all I think about—holding you, kissing

103

you—but it's *wrong*. Don't you see?"

He cupped my face in his hands, his deep-blue eyes shining in the dark. "All I see right now is you. This incredibly sweet, beautiful girl I've always admired more than anyone I know. Only, now I don't just admire you—I adore you."

He kissed me gently. I shook my head, pressing my lips tightly together. "What about Todd?" I asked bluntly.

Guilt flickered in Ken's eyes. Sighing, he lay back on the blanket. "I always thought Wilkins was the luckiest guy on earth," Ken confessed, "because he was going out with you. I didn't expect this to happen. I didn't mean to take advantage of his trust."

I nestled against his side. "What are we going to do?"

Ken rolled over to face me. "We both know what we *should* do. And we both know what we *want* to do."

"And the problem is, they're not the same thing," I whispered. He pulled my body close to his. Our lips met in a deep, searching kiss, a kiss that exploded like fireworks inside me, flooding my whole body with a fierce heat. A kiss that, for now, said it all.

Everyone knows that Jessica Wakefield is
capable of pulling some pretty outrageous
stunts! But the secrets she reveals in
Jessica's Secret Diary are like nothing
you've ever imagined. Sick and tired of
being a twin, there's nothing she won't do
to separate herself from Elizabeth. And
when it comes to getting what she wants,
Jessica doesn't play by anybody's rules. So
when she decides she's desperate for her
own sister's boyfriend, just how far will
she go? Discover the hidden life of Jessica
Wakefield in this one-time special preview
of *Jessica's Secret Diary.*

I'm so mixed up. I did something terrible to my sister today, though she doesn't know anything about it. I knew it was wrong. I never should have done it. But at the same time, I'm glad I did. Now I feel so guilty and depressed! As I said, I'm mixed up.

It's all Elizabeth's fault for being so mad at me this week. If I hadn't been mad at her for being mad at me, maybe I wouldn't have done it. But it's not fair, Diary! It's not fair that she gets to be so happy while I'm so lonely and miserable.

There. I said it. I'm lonely. Everybody else has someone. Steven and Cara. Winston and Maria. Penny and Neil. Amy and Bruce now. And even Regina and Justin. But most of all, Elizabeth and Jeffrey!!!

Jeffrey . . .

Elizabeth caught up with me at our lockers before my last-period gym class Friday.

I braced myself to be yelled at. I didn't think I'd done anything wrong, but with the way she'd been acting all week, that didn't seem to matter.

"Jessica, I'm glad I found you," she said in a rushed voice. I breathed a sigh of relief. Whatever she was up to had her in too much of a hurry to spare any time for screaming at me. "I've got to leave school right now," she said, twirling her combination lock. "Penny's out sick today, and there's a problem with *The Oracle*. I have to drive downtown to the printer's and get things straightened out."

"Elizabeth," I said with a sigh of mock martyrdom. "I really don't have time to write another last-minute article for you on bad dating experiences."

Elizabeth yanked her navy sweater out of her locker and turned on me with an impatient glare. Apparently, she was in no mood for joking around. "I just need you to track down Jeffrey to deliver a message for me before school ends today. *Do you think you can handle that?*"

I didn't like her tone, but she'd been so touchy all week that I ignored her sarcasm and tried to be pleasant. "No problem. What do you want me to tell him?"

"Tell him I'm sorry I have to break our dinner date for tonight. I won't be home from the printer's until six o'clock. I had planned to work on my Civil War paper for Mr. Jaworski this afternoon. Now I'll have to finish my rough draft tonight if I want to go to Lila's movie-watching party tomorrow. So I can't go to Tiberino's with Jeffrey."

"You're staying home to study on a Friday night?"

You would think I'd be used to Elizabeth's screwed-up priorities after sixteen years, but she still surprises me. If we didn't look exactly alike, I'd think she was left on our doorstep as an infant, by visiting martians.

"Yes, I'm staying home to study," she said, glaring at me. "But I don't want to wreck Jeffrey's evening. Tell him to go out and have a good time. I'll call him tomorrow to apologize myself and to confirm things for Lila's party."

I shrugged. "Sure. I'll tell him."

She gave me a searching look. "You won't forget?"

"You don't have to treat me like I'm six years old. I *said* I'd do it, didn't I?"

She nodded, satisfied. Then she slammed

her locker door and hurried down the hall, tossing the navy sweater over her shoulder.

My intentions were good, Diary. I was going to find Jeffrey after class and deliver Elizabeth's message. As it turned out, I didn't have to look for Jeffrey. He found me first.

I was standing at my locker in the crowded hallway after the last bell. I had just slipped on my own navy-blue cardigan when I heard a deep, sexy voice behind me and felt a warm, strong hand on my shoulder.

"Elizabeth," Jeffrey said. Then I turned to face him just in time to see his sexy smile fade. "Oh, Jessica!" he said, blushing. "I'm sorry, Jess. Your locker is right next to Liz's, and I know she wore a blue sweater today. . . ."

Normally, I hate being mistaken for Elizabeth, but it was hard to be angry at someone with beautiful dark-green eyes, thick blond hair, and the best body in the junior class. "It's OK, Jeffrey," I said with a smile, wishing he were as happy to see me as he would be to see my sister. "Actually, I'm glad you found me. Elizabeth asked me to give you a message."

I opened my mouth to tell Jeffrey that my sister had to break their date. Honest, Diary! I really did mean to tell him. But then I heard my own voice saying something entirely different. . . .

"She had to go to the printer's for *The Oracle*, but she'll be back for your dinner date. She wants you to pick her up a little early so she can get home in time to put in some work on her history paper."

"No problem," Jeffrey said with another big, sexy grin. "What's good for her? Six o'clock?"

"Make it five thirty."

At five twenty I was ready. I'd left a note on the kitchen table for Elizabeth, saying I had a date. My parents were having dinner in Los Angeles with a prospective client of my mother's, so I knew the identity of my date would remain a secret—as long as Elizabeth didn't arrive home early from the printer's.

Otherwise, I was sure I could make Jeffrey believe I was my twin. My hair was pulled back with her pearl-studded barrettes. I had on the aqua cambric dress that Heather Sanford had designed especially for Elizabeth. In my opinion the dress reached way too high on the neck and low on the legs. But its body-skimming form was flattering, the skirt twirled out nicely when I moved, and the dozens of tiny pearl buttons were more elegant than anything I owned. Also, its aqua shade made my eyes look even bluer, especially with navy mascara and eyeliner—just a tad more than Elizabeth would have worn.

I stared at myself in the mirror, and I could have sworn I saw my sister staring back. All I needed now was Jeffrey on my arm, I told myself. And I'd be magically transformed from the evil twin to the perfect twin.

When the doorbell rang, I had a moment of panic. *This isn't right!* my brain kept screaming at me. I couldn't go through with it. As I rushed down the stairs, I decided I would have to tell Jeffrey the truth.

Then he was standing in the doorway, and my resolve faded, along with the voice of conscience in my head. Jeffrey looked absolutely gorgeous. He was wearing a tweed jacket and navy pants. Through his white cotton shirt I could see a hint of color—a faint reflection of his tanned, well-developed chest. In his hand was an orchid. But it was his face that held my attention. On it was the expression he always reserved for Elizabeth. For months I'd dreamed of his green eyes looking at me that way, so full of love. And I knew I was about to have the greatest night of my life.

"You look incredible," Jeffrey said. Then he leaned forward and kissed me. It was only a quick peck on the lips, but I thought my heart would pound right out of my chest.

"Are you feeling all right?" he asked. "You look a little flushed."

"I'm feeling terrific," I said, careful to sound like my sister. "I guess I was so eager to see you that I sprinted down the stairs a little too fast."

He pinned the orchid on my dress. Even through the fabric, my skin felt as if it were burning up wherever his fingers grazed me.

Dinner was fabulous, Diary. Jeffrey was fabulous. We laughed and talked, and his eyes looked even deeper green by candlelight. Of course, I had to watch what I said very carefully. But I know my sister better than anybody. And I have a lot of practice impersonating her. When Jeffrey hit on a subject I was unsure of, it was easy to steer the conversation around so that he could supply me with the information I needed.

Luckily for me, Elizabeth had been so freaked out about Regina all week that Jeffrey didn't think it was strange for me to seem distracted.

My sister is the luckiest girl in the universe. I had never been on a date with a guy who listened to me so intently and accepted me so readily.

Jeffrey thought I looked fantastic—he said so over and over again, and I knew from the admiration in his eyes that he was sincere. But he loves Elizabeth for more than what she looks like. He loves her for what she *is* like. It took me a while to figure it out, but that's what was so different about dinner tonight. I'm used to boys who want to go out with me because I'm pretty and popular. That's all right, I guess. We have fun together. But this was different. This was special. This was what it was like to be with someone who loved me for myself. And I could almost make myself forget that it was Elizabeth he loved.

For a few minutes while we were eating cannoli for dessert, I was afraid Jeffrey was getting suspicious.

"You seem so different, tonight, Liz," Jeffrey said. His green eyes were like pools of warm water, deep enough to drown in.

I concentrated on my last forkful of cannoli. "I'm the same person I always am," I told him. "What seems different?"

He smiled. "I'm not sure. I guess you're more—*intense*."

"Does it bother you?"

"Let's just say it intrigues me."

I sighed. "I guess it's because I'm so glad to be here with you tonight—after the rotten time we've all had this week. It's all this stuff going on with Regina. I've been so uptight about her thinking I betrayed her and then turning to those awful kids for friendship." I laughed. "You should see how rotten I've been to Jessica all week. By now I think I've blamed her for everything from Regina and Bruce's breakup to the Great Depression, the Civil War, and the food in the school cafeteria!"

"She'll get over it."

"I know."

He was gazing into my eyes with such intensity that I wanted to grab him and start ripping off his clothes right there in the restaurant. I guess he was thinking along the same lines. "I know you have a paper to write," he said, "but do you have time for a stroll on the beach first?"

Warning sirens began screeching in my head, but I tuned them out. "For you, Jeffrey, I have all the time in the world."

On the beach is where it happened, Diary. I knew we shouldn't have gone there. I knew it was a bad idea. But I couldn't help myself. I've been in love about twice a month for the last five years. But this was different. This was real. And I knew that I had to see it through.

"I love walking on the beach at night," I said, dabbling a bare foot in the cool surf. Low waves rustled endlessly against the softly shining sand. The sky and water were a deep midnight-blue, with a million tiny, twinkling stars mirrored by the golden lights of boats. A seagull flew overhead, a ghostly white blur in the night.

"Me, too," Jeffrey said in a husky voice. I realized with a start that he was as breathless as I was. "As long as I'm walking with you, Elizabeth."

I could see his face in the light from the pier, and it was full of love and longing. He pulled me to his warm, strong chest and placed his lips against mine.

Oh, Diary. It was the most incredible kiss I have ever had in my entire life. A romance-novel kiss. The feelings started with my mouth and spread through my whole body so I thought I was on fire with this delirious, uncontrollable happiness. I wish I were a real writer, like Elizabeth, so I could describe it to you better. But suddenly the kiss changed. A shudder went through Jeffrey's body, and his hands tightened on my shoulders.

Jeffrey's eyes opened at the same time as mine. In them I saw the sudden realization that the twin he was kissing was not Elizabeth.

We separated, and Jeffrey looked at me wordlessly. Different emotions flashed through his eyes in that brief instant—recognition, shock, excitement, guilt, and desire. I held his gaze for a second that seemed like an hour. We both knew what we were doing, but in that second we both realized that we didn't want to stop.

Jeffrey pulled me roughly toward him again and kissed me even more passion-

116

ately. I responded with a moan, feeling as if my heart would explode with a million tiny, twinkling stars of light.

We were wrong. We knew we were wrong, but we did it anyway. And after one delicious, unforgettable minute, the guilt began creeping in until it overshadowed everything else. We pulled apart, overcome with it. Then we stared at each other wordlessly, shaking our heads.

Jeffrey and I didn't say a word to each other as we walked back to the car and drove to my house. Before I opened the car door, I looked at him and he looked at me. We still didn't talk, but we communicated just the same. Our eyes said that we both loved Elizabeth. And that we both knew our kiss this evening was the first and last one we would ever share.

And maybe—just maybe—Jeffrey regretted that fact almost as much as I did.

Look for the secret diaries of Jessica and Elizabeth Wakefield—coming to bookstores this September.

Test your Sweet Valley smarts with these games and trivia quizzes. Are you a Sweet Valley expert? Or are you still just getting to know the place? Find out right here.

Have fun!

SWEET VALLEY KIDS

1. Jessica and Elizabeth's second-grade class has a pet hamster in Book #1, SURPRISE! SURPRISE! What is her name?

2. In Book #7, JESSICA'S BIG MISTAKE, what is the name of the story that Elizabeth writes?

3. In Book #28, ELIZABETH MEETS HER HERO, Jessica and Elizabeth's class goes to see a television show being taped. What is the name of the show?

4. Where do Jessica and Elizabeth find wheels for their soap-box derby cars in Book #37, THE BIG RACE?

5. In Book #22, SWEET VALLEY SLUMBER PARTY, who is baby-sitting Elizabeth and Jessica while their parents are out of town?

6. What is Steven's award-winning science project in Book #18, BOSSY STEVEN?

118

7. Why are Jessica and Elizabeth trying to earn money in Book #9, ELIZABETH'S SUPER-SELLING LEMONADE?

SWEET VALLEY TWINS

1. What job does Jessica take to earn money to go to the Johnny Buck concert in Book #5, SNEAKING OUT?

2. What is the name of the twins' homeroom softball team in Book #17, BOYS AGAINST GIRLS?

3. What instrument is Steven learning to play in Book #46, MADEMOISELLE JESSICA?

4. Why doesn't Elizabeth want to tell Jessica who she has a crush on in Book #43, ELIZABETH'S FIRST KISS?

5. How old is Josh Angler, the boy Jessica secretly dates in Book #15, THE OLDER BOY?

6. Who is the *real* thief in Book #67, JESSICA THE THIEF?

7. What is the name of the rock band that Jessica joins in Book #34, JESSICA, THE ROCK STAR?

8. In Book #72, THE LOVE POTION, what concert tickets does Steven win?

SWEET VALLEY HIGH

1. What is the name of the cult that Jessica joins in Book #82, KIDNAPPED BY THE CULT!?

2. Jessica and Enid are competing for what honor in Book #2, SECRETS?

3. Who is Alice Wakefield with in Book #67, THE PARENT TRAP, when Jessica, Elizabeth, and Ned Wakefield run into her at Chez Sam?

4. In Book #104, LOVE AND DEATH IN LONDON, what is the real identity of Jessica and Elizabeth's roommate, Lina?

5. What is Lila's costume at her masquerade ball in Book #90, DON'T GO HOME WITH JOHN?

6. What award does Shelley Novak win in Book #55, THE PERFECT SHOT?

7. In Book #10, WRONG KIND OF GIRL, what is Annie Whitman's most desperate act?

8. What is the name of the seedy drug dealer who supplies cocaine to Regina Morrow in Book #40, ON THE EDGE?

9. In Book #100 Magna Edition, THE EVIL TWIN, how does Margo eventually die?

SWEET VALLEY UNIVERSITY

1. In Book #1, COLLEGE GIRLS, what new name does Elizabeth Wakefield's best friend, Enid Rollins give herself?

2. When Jessica decides she doesn't like sharing a room with Elizabeth in Book #1, COLLEGE GIRLS, who does she move in with?

3. What kind of flower does William White give Elizabeth the first time they speak to each other in Book #2, LOVE, LIES, AND JESSICA WAKEFIELD?

4. In Book #2, LOVE, LIES, AND JESSICA WAKEFIELD, what Elvis Presley hit becomes Jessica and Mike's "song"?

5. What expensive gift does Mike give Jessica in Book #3, WHAT YOUR PARENTS DON'T KNOW . . ., the day she moves into his apartment?

6. Who does Elizabeth suspect to be the leader of SVU's secret society in Book #4, ANYTHING FOR LOVE?

7. Where do Jessica and Mike McAllery go for their wedding dinner in Book #4, ANYTHING FOR LOVE?

To find out the answers, turn to the next page, hold the page up to a mirror, and read the reflection!

SWEET VALLEY KIDS

1. Tinkerbell
2. "The Otter's Daughters"
3. *Dr. Snapturtle's Animal Hour*
4. In the junkyard
5. Their great-aunt Helen
6. An erupting volcano
7. To buy a wedding present for their teacher, Mrs. Becker

SWEET VALLEY TWINS

1. Dog-sitting for Mrs. Bramble's dog, Sally
2. The tigers
3. The trombone
4. Because Jessica likes the same boy
5. He's sixteen, a junior at Sweet Valley High
6. Veroncia Brooks
7. NRG
8. He wins Johnny Buck tickets

SWEET VALLEY HIGH

1. Good Friends
2. Prom Queen
3. She's with Elizabeth and Jessica's English teacher, Mr. Collins.
4. She's the missing Princess Eliana.
5. Peter Pan
6. Athlete of the Year
7. She tries to commit suicide.
8. Buzz Jackson
9. She falls out of the window of Lila Fowler's pool house.

SWEET VALLEY UNIVERSITY

1. Alexandra Rollins
2. Isabella Ricci
3. A miniature white rose
4. "Love Me Tender"
5. A red 1968 Karmann Ghia convertible
6. Mike McAllery
7. Jack's Desert Rose Diner

How does your Sweet Valley trivia knowledge rate? Check your scores against our categories below to see where you stand.

A. 0-7 answers right
B. 8-16 answers right
C. 17-25 answers right
D. 26-31 answers right

A. You're a Sweet Valley novice. But don't worry, there's a simple remedy—go to you favorite library or bookstore and load up on the Sweet Valley series!

B. Nice try. You're not completely new to the world of Sweet Valley, but you have some catching up to do. Start reading!

C. Good job. You're one of Jessica and Elizabeth's dedicated fans. If you keep reading, there's a good chance you'll make it to expert.

D. Congratulations! You're a Sweet Valley expert. You know Jessica and Elizabeth almost as well as they know themselves!

This year Christmas in Sweet Valley will be more exciting than ever! Look for these four Sweet Valley Super Editions coming to bookstores in December.

Sweet Valley Kids Super Special:
TRAPPED IN TOYLAND

It's Christmas Eve, and Elizabeth and Jessica Wakefield are doing some last-minute shopping in the biggest department store they've ever seen! Then they get separated from their parents and realize the store has closed with them inside!

Being trapped alone inside toyland is a wish come true—until spooky things start happening. When the twins discover a thief is locked in the store with them, they have to figure out a way to stop him. Can they catch the thief before he catches them?

Sweet Valley Twins:
BIG FOR CHRISTMAS

Jessica and Elizabeth Wakefield have been invited to the biggest, best Christmas party of the year. They can't wait. Even high school kids will be there. They've already planned the perfect outfits when they hear the terrible news: Their parents forbid them to go. Mr. and Mrs. Wakefield insist they're too young.

The twins are absolutely furious. They go to bed that night, wishing more than anything that they were grown-ups with the freedom to do whatever they want.

The next morning, Jessica and Elizabeth wake up and discover that the most amazing thing has happened. . . .

Sweet Valley High #111:
A DEADLY CHRISTMAS

Jessica Wakefield is in danger! Finally convinced that her fiancé, Jeremy Randall, is nothing but a two-timing criminal, Jessica plots to get even. But when her devious plan goes wrong, Jessica is caught in her own trap—seconds away from a fiery death.

Elizabeth Wakefield is scared for her twin sister, and she doesn't know whom to trust. Has Jeremy's ex-fiancée, Sue Gibbons, really joined their side, or is it Sue and Jeremy against the twins? If Elizabeth's instincts are wrong, Jessica will go up in flames!

Sweet Valley University #8:
HOME FOR CHRISTMAS

Elizabeth Wakefield takes her boyfriend, Tom Watts, home for Christmas, but once they get there, memories of her old life with Todd Wilkins haunt her new romance.

Todd tries desperately to get over Elizabeth. Will Elizabeth's ex–best friend, Alexandra Rollins, help Todd forget?

Steven Wakefield lies unconscious as deadly gas fumes fill his apartment. Will Mike McAllery, the man whose life Steven ruined, save him?

SIGN UP FOR THE SWEET VALLEY HIGH® FAN CLUB!

Hey, girls! Get all the gossip on Sweet Valley High's® most popular teenagers when you join our fantastic Fan Club! As a member, you'll get all of this really cool stuff:

- Membership Card with your own personal Fan Club ID number
- A Sweet Valley High® Secret Treasure Box
- Sweet Valley High® Stationery
- Official Fan Club Pencil (for secret note writing!)
- Three Bookmarks
- A "Members Only" Door Hanger
- Two Skeins of J. & P. Coats® Embroidery Floss with flower barrette instruction leaflet
- Two editions of *The Oracle* newsletter
- Plus exclusive Sweet Valley High® product offers, special savings, contests, and much more!